M000285227

FITTING IN

AMANDA RADLEY

Sign Up to Win

Firstly, thank you for purchasing *Fitting In* I really appreciate your support and hope you enjoy the book!

Head over to my website and sign up to my mailing list to be kept up to date with all my latest releases, promotions, and giveaways.

www.amandaradley.com

FITTING IN

Silver Arches

HEATHER BAILEY SENT the email and then let out a long, heartfelt sigh. It was only ten o'clock in the morning and already her workday was looking out of control.

She stood up and looked out her office window. The Silver Arches Shopping Centre car park was filling up nicely; not bad for a weekday.

"Knock, knock."

Heather turned to see Deputy Centre Director Ravi Patel standing in the doorway, smiling as he so often did. Ravi was the best second-in-command she could have hoped for; he was a dedicated, hard worker who got on with absolutely everyone. Heather often wondered how she'd manage without him, then quickly quashed the very notion of him ever leaving her side.

"Good morning," she greeted him.

"Morning. The journalist is here." He stepped into the office, taking a healthy bite out of a red apple he held in his hand.

Heather felt her eyes widen in surprise. She'd

forgotten all about the interview she had booked for that morning.

Silver Arches was undergoing an unprecedented period of change, and she was expected to talk up what an exciting time it was. Even if, in her heart, she dreaded what was coming.

"You'd forgotten," Ravi said after swallowing the bite of fruit. He was grinning playfully, knowing full well how forgetful Heather could be.

Heather gestured to her computer. "It would have popped up on there eventually." She looked at her watch. "She's early?"

"Yes, fifteen minutes early," Ravi agreed. "I hear journalists do that to rattle people."

He was still grinning, and Heather didn't know if he was being serious or not.

"Well, I don't get rattled," Heather said, picking up her phone and clipping it to the holder on her belt.

"That's the spirit. She's by the customer services desk. I'll be with accounts if you need me; our overlords at Intrex need more figures."

Heather rolled her eyes. "Don't they always?"

They exchanged a quick farewell and headed in opposite directions. Heather moved quickly through the staff-only areas of the shopping centre, passing delivery trolleys, maintenance teams, security officers, and retail staff. Behind the public areas, Silver Arches was a community and Heather was, in many ways, their leader.

She'd come a long way since she started working in her uncle's record store all those years ago. Retail was in her blood, and Heather loved the fast-paced environment.

She exited through a large set of automatic double doors and prepared herself to be front-of-house ready. It was a theatre term, but there was a certain amount of drama in a large shopping mall such as Silver Arches.

Several sets of doors led to the staff areas, backstage and away from the guests. It wasn't unusual for employees to sag with exhaustion when returning from the centre and entering the relative calm of the staff area. Likewise, they stood a little taller when walking into Silver Arches, guest faces firmly in position.

She walked up the corridor and turned into the main thoroughfare of the centre.

Most of the stores were open or in the process of opening. Shoppers strolled around, many with a takeaway hot drink in hand, making their plans for the day.

At the customer service desk, Heather could see a young woman in a smart suit, clutching a Dictaphone as she spoke to Margaret behind the desk.

"Here's Miss Bailey now," Margaret said as Heather approached.

The journalist turned around and held out her hand. "Hi, I'm Jemma Graves from *The Echo*. Thank you so much for your time, Miss Bailey."

She shook Jemma's hand. "Thank you for coming out to Silver Arches. And, please, call me Heather."

"Are you okay if I record?" Jemma gestured to the Dictaphone in her hand.

"By all means."

Jemma pressed some buttons as they started walking. "Is that a slight accent I detect?"

Heather chuckled. "It is, I've been trying to get rid of it

3

for years. My father is from New York, but I've lived in the UK since I was six."

Jemma smiled. "My mum was born in Poland and can't shake the accent at all."

"I love the blend of cultures, languages, and accents you hear in London," Heather said. "I work with a very culturally diverse group of people, and it makes us all richer for it. Silver Arches has people from every corner of the world all under one roof, and we're very much a family here."

"A family that's about to change quite a lot," Jemma expertly turned the conversation.

"That's true. It's a very exciting time," Heather said, hoping she sounded genuine.

"The Arches Group has been reporting losses for the past three years despite owning some of the most successful shopping malls in the country. Why is that?" Jemma asked.

"Retail has been a challenging market for a few years now, due to rising property prices and costs, lower footfall. The Arches Group has been performing on a par with many of its competitors, but we know we can do better. We're in a fantastic situation to offer more to customers, and, with the help of Intrex, we are looking forward to making that a reality."

They walked along the upper floor of the centre, Heather's keen eye checking the cleaning and maintenance teams' work as they went. Thankfully, all of the silver handrails gleamed, and the glass partitions that looked down to the lower level sparkled. The marble floors and ornate lights were all spotless. It took a lot of work to keep the centre pristine, but Heather accepted nothing less.

"Is this a takeover?" Jemma asked bluntly.

"Not at all. Intrex is injecting substantial investment into Silver Arches, but The Arches Group will retain full control," Heather explained.

Both boards were keen to give the impression that the joint venture was merely two companies coming together to meet a common goal. Retail was changing, and staying ahead of that change meant investing serious amounts of cash. The Arches Group was out of money to future-proof itself from such large changes, but Intrex was an investment company with money and, supposedly, a plan.

While The Arches Group would technically be in control of Silver Arches, it wasn't lost on Heather that no investment company would throw a pile of cash at a project without wanting some say on how it was used.

She'd been in business long enough to know that what she was told by the head office and what was true were often vastly different. The higher-ups could tell her that nothing would change, but logically she knew that was impossible.

"So, the investment is limited to Silver Arches?" Jemma continued.

"Exactly. The Arches Group owns and operates seven shopping centres in the UK and three in Europe. Silver Arches is the flagship, as I'm sure you know. Situated just outside of central London, we're in an excellent location for locals and tourists. We have over two hundred thirty stores, a bowling alley, a sixteen-screen cinema, and over sixty places to eat. With free parking, you could literally spend the entire day here, and many people do."

"And with the Intrex investment? Is there any room for expansion if Silver Arches is already so big?" Jemma asked.

"Well, I can't talk about all of the exciting developments just yet," Heather said. "You'll have to wait and see, but there are big plans ahead. I can tell you that we'll be expanding our parking, and we're in talks with an exciting entertainment option."

"We did hear rumours about a virtual reality suite?" Jemma fished.

Heather smiled and shook her head. "I'm afraid I can't confirm or deny anything like that."

The truth was that nothing much had been decided. The Arches Group had thrown themselves into business with Intrex in a way that made Heather worry they were in imminent danger of bankruptcy.

Of course, she kept those concerns to herself. No one needed to see the centre director worried. It was her job to ensure that Silver Arches was running smoothly, that every shopper had a fantastic visit, and that every store felt looked-after and well maintained.

"I think I read that Silver Arches is the fifth-biggest shopping centre in the UK?" Jemma asked.

"It is, although we actually have more footfall than the fourth-biggest, so there's always a friendly debate about that," Heather said good-naturedly.

"Can we talk a little about you?" Jemma asked.

Heather blinked. "Me?"

It was supposed to be a piece about the new investment, demonstrating what a wonderful thing it was, and redirecting any concerns regarding the financial stability of Silver Arches.

She hadn't expected to talk about herself and didn't particularly want to. She'd only agreed to give the interview because she knew she had little choice in the matter.

"Yes, how long have you been centre director?" Jemma carried straight on, ignoring Heather's hesitation.

"Seven years," Heather replied, wondering how to get the interview off herself and back to the brief.

"And before that?" Jemma questioned.

"I've been with The Arches Group for nineteen years," Heather said with a wince. She wasn't exactly old, but she felt it when saying the figure aloud. "I worked my way up from a temporary summer job helping with the operations team."

"And now you're the boss," Jemma added.

"We're a team," Heather corrected gently.

Jemma nodded in a way that suggested she knew Heather was the boss and was being modest.

"Have you met Leo Flynn yet?" Jemma asked.

"We've met a couple of times," Heather answered, not wishing to be drawn into the matter if possible.

Leo Flynn, owner of Intrex, was a larger-than-life character. While he was praised for building up an investment firm now worth billions from absolutely nothing, he was also known for being opinionated, harsh, and often ruthless in his business dealings.

Heather had spent precisely one hour in the man's company, split over two thirty-minute meetings, and she felt she had a very good idea of who Leo Flynn was. Profit came first; people came second. Not Heather's way of doing business at all.

However, she did have a grudging respect for the Irishman. He knew The Arches Group inside out and was fast learning everything there was to know about Silver Arches Centre itself. He did his research, he knew business, and he could identify a good opportunity when he saw one.

Heather suspected that Leo had identified the bottom of the retail market; rents were as low as they could go following the exit of several large retailers from the marketplace over recent years.

With the big names falling like flies, smaller and more agile companies were taking over. Companies that supported a bricks-and-mortar store through an online presence were becoming the norm.

On top of that, many people were logging off from online shopping and heading back out to the shopping centres. The gloss had worn off of cheap bargains that often delivered less than they promised. People now wanted to *see* goods before they bought them.

Leo had seemingly identified the perfect time to enter the crowded market and had bought a huge stake in one of its biggest companies.

He clearly had big plans, but no one at Silver Arches was quite sure what they were yet. He played his cards close to his chest, and his brash personality meant that no one dared to question him about it.

"Will he be heavily involved in the running of Silver Arches?" Jemma asked.

"I expect we'll be seeing him now and then," Heather replied diplomatically.

Again, nothing had been decided, and the head office didn't seem to have a plan.

She'd been informed by Leo Flynn himself that she would retain her position and that he was relying on her to do exactly what she had been doing for the past seven years. But that didn't mean he wouldn't step in and upset the balance she'd created at any time he desired.

It didn't seem likely that Mr Flynn would be content to stand to one side; he surely had ideas and plans of his own. And with so much money tied up in Silver Arches, of course he would want to keep a close eye on things.

It was the unknown quantity of what her future work life would look like that kept Heather awake at night.

The board at The Arches Group had asked her to give the interview to settle any concerns that Intrex might be taking over or that rental costs might rise or that The Arches Group was in financial trouble. The problem was that Heather didn't know any of those things.

The future was looking extremely unsettled for everyone.

2

A Spy or a Test

YASMIN HELD up her hand to stop Heather in her tracks. Heather paused by her PA's desk and looked at her inquisitively, not speaking as she didn't want to interrupt the phone call Yasmin was in the middle of.

Yasmin scribbled something on a piece of paper and held it up for Heather to see.

Her eyes widened at the notification that Leo Flynn was waiting for her in her office. Heather nodded and smiled at Yasmin, grateful for the warning.

She sucked in a deep breath and walked into her office.

Leo stood by the window, hands linked behind his back, seemingly surveying all he now owned.

"Good morning, Mr Flynn," Heather greeted him. "I didn't realise we had a meeting today."

He turned around. "We didn't. I was passing on the way to the airport. Damned convenient location here for popping in when I'm travelling."

The thought made Heather's heart sink, but she tried

to swallow the emotion. The sooner she got used to Leo and his presence, the sooner it would become normal and she'd feel more settled.

She sat at her desk and picked up the post that had arrived and started to shuffle through it.

Being a successful woman in business, she knew about subtle power games and she knew exactly how to play them. She wasn't about to stand to attention at Leo Flynn's presence, nor was she going to drop everything when he randomly appeared.

She had work to do, and she fully intended to get on with her day. She suspected that Leo's unexpected visit was at least partly designed to see how she would react.

They didn't know one another other well, and they were soon going to be working with each other a great deal, both placing considerable trust in one another. They needed to figure out the other as soon as possible.

How Heather reacted now would shape their working relationship. She was taking a gamble that Leo would want her to stand up to him, would want to see that she was a strong character in her own right, and would appreciate her getting on with her work despite his unplanned presence.

"Any particular reason for popping in?" Heather asked, unfolding an invoice and checking the details as she did.

"The final paperwork has gone through. I heard from my solicitor this morning," he explained. "We're now officially in business together."

"Congratulations," Heather said and gave him what she hoped was a sincere smile.

"I thought this would be a good opportunity to talk to

you about a couple of things." He sat in the chair opposite Heather's desk.

She put her paperwork down, sensing that now was a time to pay full attention. She laced her fingers together and looked at him. "Fire away."

"Firstly, I want to talk about my, shall we say, style of management. I'm sure you've heard rumours."

Heather had. Anyone who worked in business at all had read an article or two about Leo Flynn's difficult behaviours, ability to make grown men cry, and fiery persona.

"I don't listen to rumours," Heather replied diplomatically.

He grinned, clearly not believing her but still willing to accept the lie.

"I don't suffer fools. At all," he continued. "I do my research, and my inner management team are my most trusted advisors. We like to think we know what we're talking about, and the size and success of Intrex speaks to that."

Heather nodded her agreement.

"So, when I say I want something done, it isn't up for debate. That's all I ask. I'm a fair man as long as people don't question me or think they know better than me. This is my hard-earned money and I'm investing it, which means I get to choose how it is spent." He leaned forward on his knee and pinned Heather with a stare and a grin.

"I like you, Heather. I can tell you know what you're doing. You have good people around you, you run a tight ship, and you're smart. I like that. I don't foresee us having any problems."

"Thank you, Mr Flynn. I appreciate the vote of confidence." She maintained his eye contact, another toxic business method she had learnt over the years. After a few long seconds, he nodded and sat back in the chair.

"You said there were two things?" Heather asked, eager to hurry the meeting along and prove that his little management-style speech hadn't rattled her.

"Oh yes." His face darkened a little. He shifted uncomfortably in his seat. "I have a daughter, Scarlett. I want you to find a job for her here. Anything that will keep her occupied and out of trouble."

Heather felt her eyebrow raise. She didn't think Leo and his work-hard methodology would be satisfied with just handing a job to a family member, even his own daughter.

"She's… difficult," Leo explained. "I've been looking for a place for her for a while, but I'm not too proud to admit that I've failed. We don't get on very well, so it's probably down to our personal relationship. I'm sure you'll have much more luck."

Heather swallowed nervously. Was this a test? Or some kind of trap? Was Scarlett a spy?

"I can try my best. What kind of role do you think she would be suited for?" Heather asked.

Leo threw his hands up. "Who knows? She can put her hand to pretty much anything. She's not stupid, and she's a grafter. Admin, security—hell, stick her in the canteen. Wherever you think she fits."

He looked at his watch and stood up. "I better get going if I'm going to catch my flight. I'll send Scarlett along tomorrow to see you; you can have a chat and use those leadership skills of yours to figure something out. I'll be in touch."

He was out of the room before Heather could mutter a goodbye.

She reached for her phone and called Ravi. He answered after a couple of rings, and she asked him to come to her office.

A few moments later he came in, closed the door behind him, and she told him about her brief chat with Leo.

"It's a test," Ravi said decisively.

"Perhaps. Or she's a spy," Heather added.

"Or both." Ravi paced the room. "Maybe they want us out, so she's here to report back on things and turf us out so they can bring their own people in."

"Then why congratulate me on running a tight ship and knowing what I'm doing?" Heather asked.

"Lulling you into a false sense of security?" Ravi suggested.

Despite the potentially dire situation, he was still smiling. Nothing fazed him, and Heather leeched some strength from him because of that. While she wouldn't describe herself as a bundle of nerves, she certainly did worry about things.

Ravi took everything in his stride. She imagined he could be told he had a terminal illness and was being sacked on the same day and he'd still shrug and say that other people had it worse and he'd had a great life while it had lasted. That positivity was a great source of comfort to her.

"You know someone at Intrex, don't you?" Heather asked.

"I've met a few people."

"Maybe see what you can find out? Surely the boss's daughter doesn't slip under the radar. Let's see what we can find out about her."

"Sure. What's her name again?"

"Scarlett, I presume Scarlett Flynn."

Ravi nodded. "I'll see what I can find out. I've been making friends with one of the accounts payable administrators, so I'll start there."

"Excellent. Let's see what we're dealing with."

The Robot

RAVI YANKED up the handbrake of his Mazda MX-5 sports car and grabbed his satchel from the passenger seat. He got out of the car and hurried towards the door, eager to get into the office and tell Heather everything he had discovered the previous evening.

A well-timed chat with Abigail, one of the Intrex financial controllers, had led to an invitation to a local pub with a few of the Intrex employees who had been assigned to work at Silver Arches for the foreseeable future.

"Morning, Ravi!" one of the delivery drivers, Bill, shouted over to him.

Ravi waved back. "I predict three–nil this weekend."

Bill chuckled and shook his head. "Nah, we'll knock your lot into last week! Your team is a shambles!"

Ravi laughed at the banter. He wasn't a massive football fan, but he knew enough to maintain a conversation with anyone who was. A lot of his job was speaking with people and developing relationships with them.

Asking someone to do something they didn't necessarily want to do went a lot easier if they liked you. Bill was a prime example, as he now stacked the empty pallets neatly rather than making a dangerous tower as he had done at the start of his time with Silver Arches.

"They're getting warmed up," Ravi joked.

"We'll see," Bill replied.

Ravi jumped up the short flight of steps into the building. He greeted people and picked up a coffee from the break room as he hurried to his office. Once there, he shrugged out of his coat and threw his satchel into his chair.

He exited his office and walked the few steps to Heather's. Yasmin had yet to arrive, so he invited himself in and knocked on the doorframe to his boss's office.

"Morning," she greeted him, staring at her laptop.

Heather was always the first to arrive and the last to leave. Ravi didn't know where she got the energy from.

"I have some stories to tell you," he said, closing the door behind him and taking a seat in front of Heather's desk.

Heather looked up at him and slowly closed her laptop. "Do I want to know?"

"It's about Scarlett Flynn," he said.

Heather winced. "Go on..."

"Also known as... the Robot."

Heather's eyebrow quirked. "The Robot?"

"Leo wasn't exaggerating when he said his daughter was difficult; she's had at least fifteen jobs in and around Intrex in the last three years. Ever since she was kicked out of the army."

Heather shook her head and held her hands up to slow him down. "Whoa, whoa, wait a second. Kicked out of the army?"

Ravi nodded. "She's twenty-six, was enrolled in the army at age eighteen by Leo. Was in and out like a yo-yo, from what I hear. Was suspended and disciplined multiple times before being asked to actually leave permanently three years ago."

"Who told you all of this?" Heather asked.

"Various people. I was invited to drinks last night with some of the new Intrex intake. A few beers and glasses of wine later and they spilled all these stories about Intrex, and so I subtly asked about Scarlett and, well, they had a lot to say."

Heather sat back in her chair and folded her arms across her chest. "They call her the Robot?"

"That's what they all referred to her as; apparently everyone at Intrex does. She never socialises with anyone; she's very cold and super unfriendly."

"Leo said she was difficult. Do you think he meant difficult in those terms? Socially speaking?"

Ravi took a sip of coffee before replying. "Maybe? All I can say is, she's got that interesting nickname, and nobody likes her. Oh, and they say that father and daughter don't get on at all, so I retract my theory that her coming here is a test. I think he just wants her to be someone else's problem."

Heather hummed in thought. "Or maybe it is a test. If Leo knows how difficult she is, maybe he is throwing her my way to see how I deal with her. It's just a happy bonus that he gets to palm her off on someone else."

Ravi nodded in agreement. "What are you going to do?"

Heather got to her feet and looked out the window. Ravi watched and waited. She was never one to jump into something without considering all the angles first. Heather's leadership style was thoughtful and meticulous, and Ravi had learned so much from shadowing her over the years.

"I can't give her any kind of special treatment," Heather said. "If she is some kind of test sent by Leo, he'll be looking out for if I react to her differently than I would to any other new employee coming into the fold."

"Have you thought about where to put her?"

Heather turned around. "I hadn't, but Leo did send a one-line email saying he thought, on reflection, she'd be a good fit for facilities."

"I thought he was leaving it to you?" Ravi asked.

"He apparently changed his mind." Heather shrugged. "As I told you when this whole Intrex thing started, Leo Flynn is going to want a big say in what happens around here. He may initially say that he'll leave us to it, but don't believe it for a moment. He's put a lot of money into this project, and he doesn't seem like the kind of person to hand control to someone else. Especially people he doesn't know very well."

Ravi took another sip of coffee, hoping that it would sharpen his brain before the workday officially started.

"So, facilities?" Ravi frowned. "Richard won't like that."

Richard Durkin had been the facilities manager of Silver Arches ever since there was a Silver Arches. He was a grumpy man, in a constant state of irritation about something or other. Over the years he had established a crack team of individuals who knew their roles inside out, each of them was just as moody as Richard, but their abilities allowed them to keep their jobs no matter how depressing the department as a whole was.

"No, he won't," Heather agreed. "She's coming in later this morning; I'll speak to Richard beforehand and advise him that he doesn't have much choice in the matter. Besides, he's always complaining about being understaffed."

"Can I say something terribly sexist?" Ravi asked.

Heather glared at him.

He held up his free hand to protect himself from the invisible onslaught of anger coming from Heather in waves.

"I'm sorry," he said, "but you know Richard won't like having a woman as a part of his team. Especially a young one. He'll complain."

"He can complain as much as he likes. It's happening," Heather said flatly.

"I know, I know. I'm just pointing out the obvious that old-school Richard won't like it."

Heather spread her hands in a sign of defeat. "What else can I do? Leo has requested it. Richard may have no time for office politics, but unfortunately that's what is going to keep us all in work. Leo will happily come through here and get rid of anyone who stands in his way. I, for one, am not going to end my career because I didn't follow such a simple instruction. Richard will feel the same way after I've spoken to him, I'm sure."

She sat back down again and looked at Ravi with a raised eyebrow. "Really, they call her the Robot?"

"They do."

Heather rolled her eyes. "What are we getting ourselves into?"

4

Not Very Talkative

HEATHER PICKED up her coffee cup only realising at the last moment that the final sip had already been sipped. Quite some time ago, if the stains in the enamel mug were anything to go by.

It was only ten thirty, and already it felt like a very long day.

Her phone rang, and she saw Yasmin's name flash up on the screen. She picked up the receiver and greeted her assistant.

"Scarlett Flynn is here to see you," Yasmin said professionally, indicating that Scarlett was standing right in front of her.

"Lovely, send her in," Heather said.

She hung up and stood up, smoothing down her white blouse a little. The door opened, and Scarlett walked in. Heather hadn't given much thought to what she'd look like, too preoccupied with wondering if she was a spy or a test. Now, Heather wished she had at least attempted to look her up online to prepare herself for the beauty who had just entered her office.

Heather walked around her desk and stuck out her hand. "Scarlett, it's great to meet you. I'm Heather Bailey."

Scarlett's ice-blue eyes looked at the hand with confusion for a couple of long and painful seconds before she finally grasped it with her own and gave it one solid pump before all but throwing it away.

Heather gestured towards the corner sofa in her office. "Please, sit down."

Scarlett let out a soft sigh before turning and approaching the sofa. Heather watched the tall, slim, blonde-haired woman with interest. This was the person who had apparently caused so much trouble wherever she went? The woman who had been asked to leave the military?

She looked like a stock image of a businesswoman: pretty, hair swept up in a professional up-do, dressed in a black trouser suit with a white collared shirt, with a pair of black-rimmed glasses perched on her nose.

When Leo had said that his daughter was causing him problems, Heather had expected a surly, immature woman to enter the office in torn jeans.

Scarlett sat down, perched on the very edge of the sofa and looking very much like she didn't want to be there.

Heather regarded her, realising that she didn't look bored, frustrated, embarrassed, or like any other emotion she could put her finger on. She just looked like she'd rather be anywhere else.

She looks passive, Heather realised. *Cold and aloof. I see where the nickname came from.*

Heather sat down and regarded Scarlett with a warm smile. "So, you're going to be joining the Silver Arches family?"

"Apparently so."

"I think you'll like it here," Heather said. "We're a close-knit team."

"What will my position be?" Scarlett asked.

"Your father has asked that you work with our excellent facilities team."

Scarlett took this information in with a minuscule nod of the head.

"Richard Durkin will be your line manager; he is the facilities manager here. But my door will always be open to you," Heather said, a speech she gave every new employee. "I'll also introduce you to Ravi Patel, my number two."

That didn't even receive a nod.

The silence dragged on a little.

"Do you have any questions for me?" Heather finally asked, hoping to get something out of the young woman.

"No."

Heather sucked in her cheek for a moment, wondering if she should push the woman into saying something, anything, or just leave it.

She decided to wait until another day; she had plenty of time to figure out the mystery that was Scarlett Flynn.

"Right, I can see you're eager to start work." Heather stood up and gestured to the door. "I'll give you a quick tour of the centre."

"That won't be necessary. I saw the map on the wall when I got here."

Heather paused. There was a large map just within the staff area that listed all of the stores as well as all of the operational areas of the centre.

Silver Arches was huge, and people frequently become lost. It wasn't unheard of for employees to take at least a month to find their way around without taking a wrong turn.

"Okay," Heather said. She wasn't about to waste her valuable time giving a tour to someone who didn't want it.

Scarlett would learn soon enough how big and confusing Silver Arches was, especially as she'd be working for the facilities team. "We'll pop in and see Ravi, and then I'll take you to Richard. If that's okay with you, that is?" she added the question sarcastically.

Scarlett nodded in agreement, completely ignoring the tone Heather had used.

Heather decided not to pick an argument just yet and instead gestured for Scarlett to follow her as she led the way.

Leo hadn't been kidding when he said she was difficult, and Heather was relieved that Scarlett would be out of the way, in the bowels of the building with the facilities team.

Hopefully, their paths would cross very rarely.

5

Zero Nutritional Value

HEATHER PUT the phone down and lowered her head to the desk and softly banged her forehead against the cool wood.

She'd been on the conference call for over two hours, seemingly the only voice of reason amongst the six people on the call. For some reason she was the only person who could see the problem with drilling so close to the main telecommunications lines on a Saturday when the centre was at full capacity.

Heather knew from experience that one wrong move could effectively knock out all the communications and, more importantly, payment systems for all stores in a split second.

If the engineers wanted to drill anywhere near the lines, they could do so in the middle of the night when their mistakes could be fixed before the working day started. And before Heather received complaints from over three hundred different people wondering why their connectivity had vanished.

She sat up and stretched her arms high in the air to pull out some of the tension from her spine. It was definitely time to get out of the office and get a coffee.

One of the best things about her job was the close proximity of coffee shops and restaurants. She never had to suffer through a poor cup of coffee or wonder what she'd eat for lunch or dinner.

She grabbed her purse and checked that her lanyard was still around her neck. Stepping out of her office, she glanced at Yasmin.

"Coffee?"

Yasmin's eyes lit up. "Ooh, yeah. Can I have a coconut latte?" She reached down behind her desk for her bag.

Heather waved the gesture away. "Sure, my treat."

The phone rang. Yasmin thanked her boss before answering the call.

Heather picked up her speed to get out of the office quickly in case the call was for her. No matter how important it might be, she needed coffee.

In no time she was in the public area, making a beeline for the nearest coffee shop. With a large selection to choose from, she'd not only become a coffee snob but also an expert at predicting queues at various times of the day.

As it turned out, she wasn't the only one.

"You know that has zero nutritional value, right?" she said as she came up beside Ravi, who was in the short queue, holding a plate with a particularly decadent-looking brownie on it.

"It has a pecan on top." Ravi held the plate up for her. "See?"

"Looks glazed to me," Heather replied.

"And under that centimetre of sugar is a pecan. Very healthy," he reiterated, holding it up closer for her to see.

"Oh, I stand corrected." Heather chuckled.

"Enjoy your conference call?" Ravi grinned, knowing the answer already.

"About as much as I enjoy a trip to the dentist. Did I miss anything at the operations meeting?"

They shuffled forward in the queue.

Ravi shook his head. "No, nothing important. I've sent some notes through to you. I did get a call from Richard, though."

Heather sighed. "Already?"

They moved forward again, now at the front of the queue.

"Apparently, Scarlett is already causing problems." Ravi turned his attention to the barista. "This decadent delight and a cappuccino, please. Eating in."

"And why is Richard calling you about that?" Heather asked.

"Because Richard thinks I'll be able to move Scarlett without you knowing, probably."

Heather knew it was true. Richard was old-school and didn't like having a woman in charge; nine times out of ten he'd go to Ravi instead of Heather. Not that she minded; it kept him out of her way.

However, it did annoy her that he tried to circumvent her instructions and that the main reason he appeared to do it was because he had no respect for her gender.

She walked a fine line between being happy to not have to deal with him and frustrated by his tactics. Not having to deal with him frequently won the war.

"What did you tell him?" she asked.

"I said she's nothing to do with me and he'd have to speak to you. He didn't elaborate on what the issue was. Might just be that she's sprayed body mist in the basement and offended Richard's masculine nostrils with her femininity."

Another barista looked towards Heather questioningly.

"Hi, a coconut latte and a flat white, please. Both to go."

"You know that has zero nutritional value, right?" Ravi teased.

"Caffeine is a necessary food group," Heather replied. "How did you leave it with Richard?"

"He grumbled a bit and then hung up; I didn't make any promises. Told him to speak to you and that was it. You might want to go down there and have a look around if you have time."

Heather mentally brought up her schedule for the next couple of days. "I have that meeting for the new lease in plot forty-four to prepare for, but I'll see if I can squeeze in a quick trip downstairs at some point."

The barista handed Ravi's drink over, and he thanked her.

"What did you make of her?" Heather asked.

"From the twenty seconds I saw her, not much," Ravi replied honestly. "She's quiet."

"She is," Heather agreed. "I have a feeling there's a lot more to her than that."

"There must be if she's been moved around so much,"

Ravi replied. "People don't go through fifteen jobs in three years just because they're quiet."

"Unless they are a spy and they find out what they need to find out by being quiet and then move on to the next location," Heather added softly, hoping no centre staff were around to hear her paranoia.

"Well, if she wants gossip on the inner workings of the centre, she'll need to get talkative," Ravi said. "It's my experience that people need a little gentle cajoling to give up their secrets. I don't think being quiet will cut it."

"So, maybe she's not a spy?" Heather mused.

"Time will tell," Ravi replied.

6

Keep Up the Good Work

SCARLETT FLYNN SCANNED her ID card and waited for the automatic door to slide open. She'd already noted two instances of staff leaving the security doors propped open, something she would report to security later that morning.

She'd decided to spend her first day settling into her new role at Silver Arches. Experience from her prior employers indicated that giving her own feedback on the first day of employment was rarely well received.

It was her second day, and Scarlett felt her insights would now receive the attention she knew they deserved.

She walked the long corridors and took the two stair-wells required to reach the basement level. Her direct line manager, Richard, had informed her that she would get lost in the maze beneath the centre for the first week of employment, a strange concept considering the relatively easy route which only required three turns. Signage and maps surely made it impossible for people to get lost. She had wondered if Richard had been joking with her. Not that he seemed the sort to make jokes, although Scarlett found it impossible to tell.

She put her briefcase on her desk and walked straight into Richard's office.

The surly man gawked up at her with a surprised look on his face.

"You're early."

"I wish to talk to you about the facilities reporting system," Scarlett said, standing in front of his desk.

"What about it?"

"It's inefficient."

"I'm sorry?"

"We write on sticky notes that are often not sticky enough to stick to anything. The notes are frequently misplaced, if anyone takes any notice of them at all."

Richard leaned back in his chair, folding his arms over his chest and looking at her with an expression she couldn't quite place.

"And you've ascertained all of this in less than one day? That we're inefficient? Reporting that back to Daddy, are you?"

Scarlett frowned. "My father has nothing to do with this."

"Uh-huh. Look, we've used this system for years. It works. My boys and I understand it. If it's beyond you in some way, then just say."

"Post-it Notes are not beyond me, but the system is inefficient."

"Well, there we will disagree. I suggest you get yourself a cup of coffee or whatever flavoured tea it is that you drink and get ready to man your desk. Or should I say woman your desk? Yesterday, Stevie took most of the helpdesk calls; today it will be your turn." Richard grinned in a particularly unpleasant way.

"Cocoa," Scarlett said, adjusting her glasses.

"What?"

"I drink cocoa."

Richard blinked a few times before he shook his head, sat forward, and continued reading the tabloid newspaper he'd been holding when she entered the office.

Scarlett waited a beat, checking that the discussion was over before turning on her heel and returning to her desk.

The rejection of her advice wasn't completely unexpected; she'd had experience in the past that most people took a while to take her suggestions on board. She made a mental note to approach Richard again the next morning.

She opened her bag and pulled out one of the three sachets of her preferred brand of instant cocoa. She had allocated longer to speak to Richard about her ideas for improving the efficiency of the department and was now fifteen minutes ahead of her schedule.

She hesitated for a moment, wondering if she should wait fifteen minutes now before getting her drink or get the drink now and move all of her meals and drink breaks forward fifteen minutes.

After some deliberation she took her seat, placing the cocoa sachet on the edge of her desk in preparation. She would spend the extra fifteen minutes composing an email to security to advise them of the open doors she had encountered the previous day.

Hopefully those inefficiencies would be corrected.

Several hours later, Scarlett was writing a job on a pink Post-it Note when another telephone call came in. She could tell it was for the facilities helpdesk line by the number on the screen.

She picked up the receiver and answered the call in the exact manner Stevie had taught her.

"Hi, it's Grace from The Gift Box. There's been a spill in the doorway, some soft drink. I need someone to come and clean it up immediately."

"What is your store number?" Scarlett asked.

"One hundred and seventeen, on the top floor by the main elevator. When will someone be here?" Grace asked.

"I don't know," Scarlett replied honestly. "I will have to write out a green note and wait for someone to pick it up."

"A green note? Can't you call someone? This *is* urgent, you know," Grace asked, an edge to her voice.

"No. I have to wait for someone to pick up the green note. I have advised them that it is an inefficient system."

"Look, I need you to speak to someone immediately. It's a big spill; there are ice cubes. Someone will fall and hurt themselves. I need someone here immediately. This is a serious hazard."

Scarlett frowned. "If it's as hazardous as you claim, then maybe you should clean it up yourself?"

"Excuse me?"

"I said, if it's as hazardous as you claim, then maybe you should clean it up yourself," Scarlett repeated.

"That's not my job," Grace replied.

"But you say it's an immediate danger to guests, in which case you should clean it up yourself. Do you wish to cancel your request and take ownership of the spill yourself?"

"No, I want you to do your damn job and get someone here as soon as possible," Grace said, her voice presenting a strange tone.

"Then I will write a green note and wait for someone to pick it up. Goodbye."

Scarlett hung up the call. She picked up a stack of green Post-it Notes and wrote the relevant details and pinned it to the board.

Richard walked back from a meeting he had been attending and glanced at the board. He lifted his glasses and looked at the newly affixed green note.

"That doesn't go there," he said.

"I was told that cleaning requests go on a green note on this board in this column," Scarlett said.

"Ordinarily, but this is a spill. It's a health and safety issue." He ripped the note from the cork board. "Hey, Kaz!"

Karen Saunders from the cleaning department in the next room shouted back. "What?"

"Spill outside Gift Box, love," Richard shouted.

"I'll get Kath up there, thanks!"

Scarlett looked at Richard in surprise. "This system was not explained to me. I am supposed to contact the cleaning department directly if there is a spill?"

"Depends where it is," Richard said. He screwed up the piece of paper and threw it in a nearby bin.

"Do you have an example of when I do and when I do not call the cleaning department?" Scarlett asked.

"No, you use your head," Richard replied, tapping the side of his head with two fingers. "Common sense."

He brushed past her and entered his office, slamming the door behind him.

Scarlett winced. She glanced at the cork board and removed the pin and the scrap of green paper that had remained in place after Richard removed the rest. She put the scrap in the bin and put the pin back in the central pin pot.

She returned to her desk and opened up the document she had been working on. It listed all the recommendations she had for improving efficiency in the facilities department.

Scarlett sipped at her three o'clock cocoa. The kettle in the staff room didn't make the water as hot as she'd like. Like other things in the department, it was half-hearted in its application to its central role in life.

"Ah, there you are."

Scarlett turned around and regarded the centre director, Heather Bailey, with a raised eyebrow. "Yes, this is my desk."

Heather hesitated a second before walking up to Scarlett and perching on the edge of her desk.

"How are you settling in?" Heather asked.

"I have yet to get lost, despite the assumption from everyone that I will," Scarlett replied.

"That's good. I had a call from Grace O'Connor this afternoon. She wasn't very happy," Heather explained.

"I also spoke to Grace this afternoon," Scarlett said.

Heather expelled a breath. "Yes, I know. Her call to me was after she'd spoken to you. You see, Grace is the kind of woman who likes to complain. And when she does that, she goes straight to the top."

"You," Scarlett surmised.

"Me," Heather agreed.

"She wished to complain about me?" Scarlett asked. She quickly replayed the conversation she had had with Grace and couldn't find any fault in it.

"Yes, apparently she didn't like your attitude," Heather explained.

"I didn't like her attitude either," Scarlett assured Heather.

"Well, in this situation, Grace is a customer of ours. You run a helpdesk and you need to be respectful when you speak to her. Or anyone who calls the helpdesk."

"I was respectful."

"She says you hung up on her."

"I'd finished talking."

Heather pinched the bridge of her nose and expelled some more air.

"The spill was cleaned," Scarlett added. "Richard expedited the request by shouting to the cleaning department. It is not very efficient."

"Look, I'm in a bit of a hurry." Heather slid from the desk and smoothed her trousers. "Just try to be nicer and more respectful when tenants call. Don't hang up on them, and don't suggest they clear up spills themselves. That's what they pay us to do."

Scarlett nodded.

"Great, keep up the good work." Heather started to leave.

"You've just complained about my work," Scarlett pointed out, spinning her chair to regard Heather curiously.

Heather paused and slowly turned to face her.

"I…" Heather shook her head. "Yes, I did. I suppose I meant to say, do better work."

"I'll endeavour to follow these new rules," Scarlett reassured her.

"Right. Great. Well, I'm running late. I have to go."

Scarlett watched her leave before turning back to her desk. She picked up her mug of cocoa and winced at the tepid temperature.

7

Nico and the Pop-Up

RAVI PULLED up in his car outside the bookshop and put the car into park. He picked up a bundle of paperwork from the front seat and exited the vehicle.

A bell announced his arrival into Gay Days Books, and Nico Frazier looked up from the counter.

"Ravi!" she greeted him enthusiastically.

"Hey, Nico. How are you?" Ravi asked, looking around the small bookstore.

"I'm good. I'll be even better if you have good news for me?" Nico leant on the counter and looked hopefully up at him.

Ravi waved the paperwork in front of her. "You mean, did I manage to get you a pop-up location in one of the biggest shopping centres in London? Of course I did!"

Nico screeched happily and jumped up and down on the spot. "Really? Like, really?"

"Really," Ravi confirmed. "You better call some of your staff because very soon, you'll be running two venues."

Nico looked around the shop with wild, excited eyes.

"I'm totally taking the badges and the postcards. People love postcards. How rude can they be? Some are a bit risqué."

Ravi chuckled and put the papers on the counter. "Everything you need to know is in here. As long as the rude merchandise isn't too prominently displayed, you'll be fine."

"How can I ever thank you for this?" Nico asked.

"Nothing to thank me for," Ravi said. "I'm glad these pop-ups will provide some diversity to the centre. And who doesn't need more LGBTQ books in their lives?"

"Is that gorgeous boss of yours still single?" Nico asked, waggling her eyebrows.

"Heather? Yeah, since she ended things with her ex three years ago." Ravi flipped through a stack of home-made greetings cards on a stand on the counter. "Doesn't seem to be interested in dating, and she's married to her job."

"Oh, I'm not interested in her like that," Nico explained. "She's nice to look at, you know, from afar. Just don't want to be knocked out by her girlfriend, if she had one."

Ravi shook his head. "Now, if I said that about a woman I would probably be in trouble."

"Yep, you'd be a pig."

"But you can?" Ravi chuckled.

"Yeah, of course. I'm adorable and harmless," Nico told him with a grin. "I'm delightful."

"That you are," Ravi agreed.

Ravi had met Nico at a bar one night many years

before when he was accompanying his newly out cousin to his very first gay bar.

They'd hit it off immediately, both working in retail and sharing stories of crazy customers and unreliable suppliers.

Nico had established the raggedy bookshop when her grandmother had passed away and left her a small inheritance. The store didn't make much money, so Ravi did what he could to publicise and help the small business.

When Heather had mentioned a project working with the local council to bring small, independent stores into Silver Arches in temporary pop-up stores, Ravi had instantly thought of Nico.

When the project approvals had come through, Ravi knew he had to let Nico know in person. Mainly because if he'd done it via telephone, the scream of excitement may have permanently deafened him.

Ravi tapped the lollipop box. "Won't be able to bring these. No free lollipops."

Nico looked shocked. "Really?"

"Yep. Health and safety. We'd need you to be certified to handle food, and then—"

Nico held her hand up. "I get it, no lollipops. Fine. But you're not taking away my stickers." She grabbed a large reel of rainbow stickers and held it to her chest. "Over my dead body."

Ravi laughed. "You can keep your stickers, I promise."

An hour later Ravi drove into the main car park of Silver Arches. The rain had started falling hard not long after he left Nico's place, and his windscreen wipers were struggling to keep up with the deluge.

"What on earth…"

Someone was standing in the car park in a neon-yellow, high-visibility jacket and trousers. On busy days, a team of parking assistants would guide traffic through the large parking spaces that surrounded Silver Arches. With a mixture of parking garages, underground parking, and surface parking, the centre sometimes became congested on busy days, and assistance was needed to keep everything safe and in order.

But it was the middle of the week and there was no need for a parking assistant to be out.

Whoever was hidden by the large hood was gesturing for him to turn left, down the only path available to him. It seemed like a pointless endeavour.

He slowed the car and opened the window as he pulled up alongside them.

"Scarlett?" he asked, barely recognising her. She may have been wearing the high-visibility jacket complete with hood, but that hadn't stopped the torrential rain from soaking her face. Her glasses were fogging up, and strands of blonde hair were stuck to her face.

"What are you doing out here?" Ravi shouted over the sound of the rain hitting the ground.

Scarlett stepped closer to the car. "Richard thought I could do with some work experience with the parking team."

"Okay, and who sent you out here in this weather?"

"Luke," Scarlett said, referencing the parking garage manager.

Ravi cursed under his breath. "We don't need you out in the car park today, especially not in this weather. Head back to the parking office. I'll meet you there."

Scarlett gave him a quick nod and started walking back towards the building. He was sure he could hear squelching from her boots and belatedly realised he should have offered her a lift in the car. He looked up, but she was too far away on the pedestrian path to call her back.

He closed the window and hurriedly drove towards his spot. The pedestrian path meant that Scarlett would have to go the long way around and Ravi had a direct route.

Grabbing his umbrella, he hopped out of the car and rushed into the parking office. Luke and two of the parking attendants were sitting around, drinking coffee and laughing.

"Why is Scarlett Flynn outside in this weather?" Ravi demanded.

"We're inefficient," Luke said, his arms wide in a gesture of incredulity. "She'd been down here for all of ten minutes. I explained to her how we feed the car park during busy periods. She said I was wrong. I asked her to elaborate, and she, who has never done this before, says she has a better way. Ten years I've been in traffic management. Ten years."

"It's torrential rain out there," Ravi pointed out, not at all interested in the office politics that had led to her being sent outside.

"She's got protective clothing on. If it were a weekend, we'd all be out in this weather. She's not getting special treatment from you because she's the boss's daughter, is she?" Luke challenged.

"Of course not. No one *needs* to be out there today," Ravi argued. "If I saw Pete out there, I'd send him in."

"I didn't technically order her out there; I just asked her to explain what she meant," Luke said, a cocky smile on his face.

Pete burst out laughing. "You should have seen her, Ravi. She was trying to explain to us a better way to do things. Saying that we should do this. We're inefficient. That kinda thing. So, we play dumb. Pretend we don't get what she's saying."

Luke started to laugh. "She's getting more and more frustrated, so I said to 'go out and show us.' She got her all-weather gear on and went out there. Idiot."

"What's she doing here anyway? She's meant to be with Richard," Ravi said.

"He got sick of her. Something about Post-it Notes. I said I'd take her for the afternoon in exchange for a beer," Luke said.

Ravi ran a hand through his hair. Heather was going to flip out when she heard. It wasn't lost on Heather that a lot of the operational aspects of the business were dominated by men who had been in their roles for a very long time. Many of them didn't want to change their ways and a 'boys' environment' had definitely developed.

Ravi and Heather were working to try to change things, but without mass firings it was a slow process.

Scarlett entered the office and pushed her hood back.

"As you can see, allowing traffic to cross departing lanes is inefficient. Using lane one as an exit instead of as coach parking would clear any potential overcrowding," she said. "As well as improve visibility on what otherwise would be a blind corner."

"Where do we put the coaches?" Luke asked smugly.

"Lane thirty-two," Scarlett replied immediately. She tilted her head towards Luke, inviting his next comment.

Luke opened and then closed his mouth a couple of times, seemingly unable to come up with an appropriate response.

"We'll revisit this later," Ravi said. "Scarlett, get out of those clothes and get dry and then go back to facilities. I'll tell Richard to expect you."

Scarlett looked like she was about to argue but instead offered a clipped nod and walked out of the room.

"No more pranking the new person," Ravi told Luke. "I don't care who they are or how annoying they are. And certainly not in exchange for a beer. I'm going to have to report this to Heather."

Luke rolled his eyes.

Ravi didn't bother to say anything else; he knew his words would be lost on Luke and his staff. If Luke wasn't interested in adjusting his ways and keeping his job, then Ravi wouldn't be able to help him anyway.

8

Where Next?

HEATHER EXITED the conference room and walked to the exit with the property team from Happy Senses Perfumes. It had been an excellent meeting, and Heather was reasonably confident they would choose to rent the empty shop space.

She said goodbye to them in the reception area, aware that Ravi was conspicuously hanging around. It was clear that he wanted to speak to her once she was alone.

The only time he did that was when there was an issue that he needed to discuss with her; rarely was it good news.

Once the meeting attendees had all left, she turned to look at her second-in-command. "Problem?"

"Scarlett Flynn," he said softly so people didn't overhear.

Heather resisted the urge to roll her eyes and gestured for him to follow her to her office, where they could have a private discussion about their newest member of staff.

They entered Heather's office, and Ravi closed the door behind them.

"I got back from delivering the paperwork to Nico and saw Scarlett in the car park," Ravi said.

Heather sat down and looked at him with a raised eyebrow. "What do you mean?"

"In full hi-vis, in the pouring rain, guiding traffic. Which was only me because it's a quiet period." Ravi took his customary seat in front of her desk. "Richard had exchanged her for a beer."

Heather felt her anger bubbling. "Say that again."

"I don't have all the details—I suspected that you might want to deal with this personally—but as far as I understand it, Richard got fed up with her and asked Luke to take her for an afternoon. Scarlett seemed to think she was getting work experience with the parking team. Richard just wanted an afternoon of peace and quiet, and Luke agreed."

"For the price of a *beer*?" Heather clarified.

"Yes. Apparently, Scarlett has a thing about efficiency. She immediately told Luke that they were doing things wrong, had a much better idea on how to run the whole operation."

Heather smothered a smile behind her hand. "Oh. I bet Luke loved that."

Ravi grinned. "Not much. But he got his revenge by sending her out in the rain to prove her point."

Heather shook her head. "You're right, I do want to deal with this myself. Are you really telling me that two grown men can't cope with a young woman? That they have to trade her for beer?"

Ravi removed a slip of paper from his inner jacket pocket and handed it over.

"What's this?" Heather asked as she unfolded the paper.

"Scarlett's CV. I managed to get a copy from HR. I don't know why Leo wanted her in facilities, but I'd say she might be a better fit in security."

Heather looked over the résumé. It appeared, as Ravi had suggested before, that Scarlett had moved from school straight into the army. No explanation was given on the CV for why she left her military career.

Following that, she had rapidly gone through a number of departments in Intrex Investments.

"Why does she keep getting moved on?" Heather wondered out loud.

"From what I understand, she's difficult. She doesn't want to do things the way people ask her."

"You said she told Luke that he was doing things wrong?" Heather clarified.

"Yes. She seems to like calling people inefficient," Ravi said.

The phone on Heather's desk rang its specific tone, indicating an internal call. She sat forward and noticed it was Yasmin calling from the outer office. She picked up the phone.

"Richard from facilities is here to see you," Yasmin said.

"Send him in." Heather hung up the call and looked at Ravi. "Richard's here. Let's get some answers."

Richard entered the office. He looked as grumpy as ever; he also looked like a man who was about to defend his actions, which Heather found laughable, considering she already had the insider knowledge on what he had done and why.

"We were just talking about you," Heather said. "Come in, close the door, and take a seat."

Richard grumbled under his breath but did as he was told.

"As her manager, I think I have the right to choose if she needs extra training in a certain area," Richard complained. Rather boldly, Heather thought.

Ravi laughed. "Nice try, Luke already told me you got sick of her and exchanged her for a free drink at the pub."

Richard's eyes widened, and he snapped his head towards Heather.

"You don't know what she's like; she's a nightmare," he explained. "She will only answer the call on the third ring. Ever. She complains about how sticky Post-it Notes are. She doesn't *get* the most basic thing, like if a light is flickering in the elevator it needs to be replaced immediately before some poor sod has a seizure. She has the audacity to try to change the way we do things when she doesn't even understand half of what we do."

Heather held her hand up to silence him. "Why didn't you come to me, or Ravi, with this? Why trade her like a commodity?"

"If I came here and told you I couldn't handle a little girl—"

"Fully grown woman," Heather corrected tersely.

Richard shrugged. "Well, yeah, that. It wouldn't look good, would it?"

"Neither does this, to be honest," Heather said, punctuating her sentence with a sigh. "Where is she now?"

"Getting a new kettle," Richard said.

Heather narrowed her eyes and gave Richard her iciest stare.

"She wanted to get one!" Richard defended himself quickly. "She said ours was only 'achieving a minimal boil,' and it meant her cocoa was cooling too quickly."

"Cocoa?" Heather blinked.

"That's what she said. Anyway, she was whining about it, so I told her to get a new kettle with money from petty cash." Richard folded his arms across his chest. "I don't like having a spy in my facilities office."

"She's not a spy," Ravi said.

"Isn't she? All this talk about efficiency makes me think she is," Richard argued.

"Maybe you're just so inefficient she can't help herself?" Ravi teased.

Heather tuned out their bickering and thought about the woman at the centre of all of this. It was clear that Richard couldn't cope with her. And Heather couldn't begin to imagine the toxic environment that Scarlett was currently being asked to work in.

Whether she was a spy or not was still up for debate. Scarlett didn't act like a spy. Spies fitted into their environment in order to gather information and report back. They didn't stick out and loudly complain about kettle boiling temperatures.

Heather knew that Intrex had its own efficiency monitors. The team were sent into new acquisitions to find issues with working practices and decide what fat could be cut. If Scarlett was one of them, surely Leo wouldn't have been so sneaky about deploying her.

But if she wasn't a spy, she could still be a test. Was Leo using his notoriously difficult daughter to see if Heather's leadership skills were up to scratch? And, if so, what would be seen as weakness?

Would pulling Scarlett out of facilities be viewed as not being able to control Richard and his archaic management style? Or would it be seen as identifying a mismatch and being brave enough to fix the problem regardless of what it looked like from the outside?

And that was all *if* it was a test. Which Heather didn't know for certain.

All she did know was that Scarlett was quickly turning into her problem.

"Okay," she said, interrupting the two men and their squabble. "I'm pulling her out of facilities. It's obviously not a good fit. For either party."

Richard looked unbearably smug. Heather itched to do something to wipe the grin from his face, but she wouldn't. He could think he had won; it wasn't relevant in the grand scheme of things. Picking her battles was essential to good management.

"Put up with her for the rest of the day," Heather instructed. "Clearly she's bested you after a few short days, so I'll have to place her with someone who can cope."

"Now, wait a minute," Richard argued. "No one said I couldn't cope with he—"

"You did through your own actions," Heather told him firmly. "Now, I won't discuss it anymore. Go. Ravi will come and see her later and discuss the details of the situation with her."

Richard looked like he wanted to defend himself further, but one glare from Heather had him rethinking that choice.

Once he was gone, Ravi raised an eyebrow.

"What's the plan, boss?"

"You said she might fit better in security," Heather said, picking up the CV and glancing through it again. "I'm inclined to agree. And Tara will no doubt be able to cope with her better than Richard or Luke can."

Tara Manning had been the head of security at Silver Arches for just over twelve months. She was a force of nature, disciplined, efficient, a great leader, and someone Heather had complete faith in.

If she'd had sight of Scarlett's CV beforehand, she probably would have put Scarlett in security anyway. She couldn't fathom why Leo had suggested facilities unless it was simply to keep her out of the way. Maybe Leo employed an 'out of sight, out of mind' mentality when it came to his daughter.

"Sounds like a plan," Ravi agreed. "Will you speak to Tara, or shall I?"

"I'll do it," Heather said. "I have some things to discuss with her anyway. You go and see Scarlett and let her know to report to Tara first thing tomorrow. Oh, and try to… I don't know, get to know her. Talk to her, use some of your charm to figure out what she's about."

Ravi chuckled. "My charm?" He looked like he had no idea what she was talking about, but Heather knew better. Ravi was known for his good looks and his charisma.

Heather pointed at his face. "Yes, use that cheeky smile. Try to get through to her. We need to know more about her if we're going to make this work, for her and for us."

"I'll do my best," Ravi promised.

"Do. We don't want to find out she *is* a test... after we've failed it."

9

A Problem Solved

HEATHER KNOCKED on the open door to the security office. Tara Manning looked up and smiled warmly.

"Hello, to what do I owe this honour?" Tara gestured for Heather to come in and take a seat.

"I have a favour to ask," Heather confessed as she sat down.

"You want me to take on the new girl that no one else wants?" Tara assumed.

Heather chuckled. She should have known that stories of Scarlett would have spread around the centre like wildfire. Everyone loved to gossip, and Scarlett provided them with a lot of it. Anyone with their ear to the ground, such as the security manager, would no doubt have heard all about Scarlett Flynn by now.

"I actually think she'd be a good fit," Heather said, trying a different avenue of approach. "She's ex-military, has a very keen eye for detail. She's fit and healthy. No nonsense. Hard worker."

Tara simply grinned at Heather.

"Is any of this working?" Heather asked good-humouredly.

"I don't know, keep trying," Tara joked.

Heather flopped back in the chair. "Don't make me beg."

Tara grinned some more. "Is she as bad as people say she is?"

Heather seriously considered the question for a moment. The truth was, she didn't really know.

Scarlett wasn't the easiest person to speak to, that was for sure. Why that was and what was behind it were a mystery to Heather.

Putting Scarlett in the basement with Richard had been a bad idea; the facilities team as a whole wasn't well known for their ability to cope with changes in management or personnel.

It was entirely possible that the two things combined to create a bad start for Scarlett. Maybe things would have been better if she had been placed in the right department at the beginning.

"I don't really know her," Heather admitted. "I do know that she seems to be a hard worker and dedicated. But she's not the most personable of people; she's not easy to talk to. At all, from what I gather."

"I can work with that," Tara said, "but she won't get any special treatment because she's the boss's daughter. So, if she thinks that, she'll have to think again."

Heather shook her head. "I don't think she's like that. She doesn't seem close to her father."

Tara frowned. "Then why is she here? Aren't we

handing her any job she wants on a platter just because of who her daddy is?"

"Technically. But there doesn't seem to be much of a connection between the two of them from what I can make out," Heather explained.

She couldn't imagine not having a relationship with her own father. Mike Bailey was her hero; he'd always been there for her no matter what. They'd clashed a little when she was growing up and she had entered her awkward teenage rebellion stage, but it hadn't lasted long. Before long she was back to being daddy's little girl, or 'Pumpkin' as he fondly called her.

While she knew not everyone had the happy connection she had with her parents, Heather thought that it must have been a very lonely existence for Scarlett to not have a close relationship with her father, especially when they had the opportunity to work side by side if they chose.

"That's a shame," Tara said. "Well, I'm happy to take her on. I'm recruiting anyway, so it's great timing as we'll have a new intake soon. Training in batches is far more efficient."

And Scarlett loves efficiency, Heather thought to herself.

"Keep me in the loop, and if there any problems please let me know directly. I don't need to be blindsided by Leo Flynn if anything is up."

"I'll keep you updated," Tara reassured her.

Heather took a sip of red wine, having just enjoyed a splendid meal for one in the comfort of her own home, at a reasonable time for a change.

Being in charge had its highs and lows. One of the lows was that she spent more time at work than she did at home, which was a shame, because she loved her small apartment.

In her off time, Heather was spoilt for choice of things to occupy her. Her list of television shows to watch had enough on it to entertain a person for fifty years; her music collection was full to bursting and yet hardly ever enjoyed. It was no secret that she enjoyed logic puzzle books and received them from loved ones on most birthdays and Christmases. They now filled in the gaps in an already overflowing bookshelf.

Yet most of the time she simply turned on the news and drank a glass of red wine. It was a pattern she'd gotten into long ago, and she longed for the day when she'd have more time to herself. However, she knew in her heart that time would only come if she made it a priority.

Living alone meant it simply wasn't one.

It wasn't that Heather didn't want a relationship. She did, but the right person always seemed to elude her.

She'd dated, even been in what could be considered serious relationships, but she'd always known that the person she was with wasn't 'the one'.

She stuck with these relationships, assuming they were was as good as it was going to get. The idea of fitting perfectly with someone seemed like a fanciful movie plot, and so Heather assumed such things didn't exist.

That didn't stop her from longing for some companionship from time to time.

Her work phone rang, and she winced at Leo Flynn's name on the screen. He didn't seem to be a man who kept normal office hours, and he had recently decided to sidestep The Arches Group chain of command and directly work with Heather on all things related to Silver Arches.

She answered the call.

"I'm having a letter sent out to Marco's and Zanzibar. Those two restaurants have the highest footfall and they haven't had a rent rise in over two years," Leo said, getting straight to the matter at hand.

"Okay. You're upping their rent?" Heather guessed.

"Yes, in six months' time. Just to put them in line with the other restaurants' square-meterage costs," he continued.

Heather could understand why, but she did wonder about the logic of potentially upsetting two very large chain restaurants.

"If they come whining to you," Leo continued, "let me know."

"I will most certainly do that," Heather promised. She had no intention of taking on that particular battle and would happily pass on any complaints to the man who had made the decision to rock the boat.

"Great, the letter will be with them in the morning."

"I'll let you know if I hear anything," Heather said. "By the way, Scarlett is being moved to security. I think that's going to be a better fit for her expertise."

"Yes, whatever. I do need to grab ten minutes with you to talk about the old management offices on the third floor at the south end. That is dead space, and we need to come up with some ideas for that."

Heather bit her lip. She wanted to push on the Scarlett matter, but it was very clear that Leo had no interest in the topic.

"Okay, I'll check my diary—"

"I'll swing by," Leo said with finality before hanging up the call.

Heather lowered the phone and stared at her home-screen photo of herself and her parents. "And I'll let you know when I have some time to discuss that, Mr Flynn," she finished to herself.

The photo of her parents made her smile. Without a second thought, she pressed some buttons and called her father.

It only took a couple of rings before he answered, "Hey, Pumpkin."

"Hey, Dad," she replied, feeling a smile taking over her face. It felt good to talk to him, even if it had only been a couple of days since they last spoke.

"How are you, honey?"

"I'm good," Heather said.

"Is that new boss of yours treating you well?" Mike Bailey always had a way of knowing exactly what was going on in Heather's life without her having to say a word.

"He's… okay," Heather admitted. "I've had to deal with way worse."

"Don't let him get you down," Mike instructed.

"I won't, Dad," Heather promised. "But I didn't call to talk about work. How are you? How's Mum?"

"We're good. I got that quote for the work up on the second barn."

Heather could tell from his tone that it wasn't a good quote.

"Expensive?" she asked.

"Just need to sell your mother's kidneys," he joked. "Maybe a leg."

"Are you sure we can't do it ourselves?" Heather asked.

It had been a while since she'd had a project to work on with her father. Between them, their DIY skills were pretty impressive. She'd spent most of her childhood eagerly helping her father with any home maintenance project he'd taken on.

As a young girl, she'd watch him eagerly and handed him whatever tools he called for. As she got older, she was entrusted with some basic tasks. By the time she was eleven, she knew how to put up shelves and fix floorboards. It was a skill set that had come in handy throughout her life.

"Maybe," Mike said. "I know you're busy, honey."

"Not too busy to come and help you," she reassured. "Maybe get the professionals in for some of it and we can take on the rest?"

He sucked in a thoughtful breath, weighing the options.

"I mean, we can put together some plywood easy enough, can't we?" she added, hoping to convince him.

A project away from work was just what she needed, something she could really get her teeth into; a good reason, other than seeing her folks, for spending some time back on the farm.

It would be good to be shoulder to shoulder with her dad again, before he got too old to take on such tasks.

"Why don't you come down and take a look?" Mike suggested. "So you know what you're agreeing to take on. It could be quite a few weekends of work."

"I'm up for it," Heather reassured him. "I'll see when I have a weekend free to come down."

"It will be great to see you, honey. Oh, did I tell you about Ralph Long and that old tractor of his?"

Heather reached for her glass of wine and leaned back into the comfort of the sofa. She closed her eyes and listened to her father's voice wash over her.

10

Inefficiencies

RAVI ENTERED the facilities office and paused in the doorway. Scarlett was standing in front of the pinboard used for monitoring reporting issues and applying pins to each of the corners of the coloured square notes.

Each note was pinned exactly straight and with an equal amount of space surrounding it. Some would consider it artistic.

Ravi took a step into the room and applied his biggest smile to his face.

"Hey, Scarlett," he greeted her.

Scarlett looked at him over her shoulder and gave him a single nod. She then turned her attention back to the pinboard and adjusted the remaining notes.

Silence stretched on for a few seconds, and Ravi realised that Scarlett wasn't about to stop what she was doing or even glance at him again.

"Um. Can we have a little chat?" he tried again.

"About what?" Scarlett asked, still focused on her task.

Ravi chuckled to himself. As a member of senior

management, he was used to people giving him their full attention and not questioning him when he wanted to talk. It seemed that Scarlett wasn't interested in him or what he had to stay, certainly not if it interrupted her project at hand.

"Maybe we could take a seat?" Ravi suggested.

That seemed to work. Scarlett paused, a pin in her hand just about to land in the exact corner of a pink piece of paper. She took a step back and dropped the pin into a pot, still looking at the board. Finally, she pulled her gaze away from it and looked at Ravi expectantly.

He gestured to Scarlett's desk and pulled up a chair of his own, placing it by Scarlett's. She sat down and looked at him with a passive expression.

"I've been speaking with Heather," Ravi said, "and we think you'd be a better fit with the security team. What do you think about that?"

She nodded and pointed to her desk. "Should I pack my things?"

Ravi looked at the notepad, pen, mug, and coaster which lay on the desktop, arranged perfectly. He shook his head. "Not yet. I'm interested to hear if you think that security might be a better fit for you."

"I've never worked there," Scarlett replied. "I have no thoughts on whether or not it might be a better fit."

Ravi had to admit she had him there.

"Okay, well, yes, that's true," he agreed. "But do you *think* that it might be a better fit?"

"If I'm to be moved anyway, is it relevant what I think?" Scarlett asked.

Ravi flinched slightly. The cold, harsh tone was not

one he expected from an employee, but he had quickly learnt that Scarlett wasn't the average employee.

"It's always relevant what you think," Ravi stated.

"I disagree." Scarlett gestured to the pinboard. "I have explained to several people why the pinboard system is inefficient and no one is interested."

"People don't like change," Ravi explained. "Or being told they are inefficient."

"*They* are not inefficient; the system is," Scarlett explained. She tilted her head to one side as she considered her words. "Except Tom. He is inefficient."

Ravi had to agree. Tom, affectionately called Old Tom, was completely useless and only allowed to stay out of kindness, as his retirement date was just a few months away.

Ravi wasn't about to get into that discussion with Scarlett. While he was now quite sure that Scarlett wasn't a spy planted by Leo, he didn't know with absolute certainty. He also somehow suspected that Scarlett wouldn't fully understand the decision that had been taken regarding Tom.

"People don't like being told their systems are inefficient either," Ravi said. "Maybe you should try another approach? Maybe instead of pointing something out as inefficient, you should say you have a way that might work better?"

Scarlett seemed to consider this before nodding her agreement.

"Should I pack my things now?" she asked.

Ravi realised that attempting to connect with Scarlett was going to be a lot harder than he thought. His apparently charming smile was doing nothing to dent the wall Scarlett had around her.

"If you like," he agreed. "Report to the security office tomorrow morning at nine; they'll be expecting you. It's on the upper floor with the management suite. You need to go through the main doors, and then tur—"

"I know where it is."

"Oh, you've been already?"

"No. I just know where it is." Scarlett picked up her pen and clipped it to her notebook.

"Have you had a chance to make any friends since you started here?" Ravi asked, even though he was already sure he knew the answer.

"No."

"There's a few social clubs; you should check out the intranet. People often meet in the local pub after work. And there's a movie club who go to the cinema every Wednesday. You know we get discounts from the cinema onsite, right?"

Scarlett put her notebook in her bag. "Thank you, I will look into it."

Ravi got the distinct impression that she wasn't going to look into it at all. He wondered if he should invite her directly to the next pub meet-up, try to force her out of her isolation and get her to mingle with the more sociable employees in the centre.

He decided to allow her some time to do so herself before he became involved. It wasn't up to him to force people to socialise if they didn't want to, even if he did think it would help them.

"Okay, well, if you need anything, you know where I am." He stood up.

"Level two, management suite, room fourteen," Scarlett replied.

"Er… yeah. That's where I am," Ravi said.

Scarlett gestured towards the board behind Ravi. "Are we finished? Can I complete my work?"

"Sure." Ravi stood up and wheeled the spare chair back to where he had found it. Scarlett returned to the pinboard, picking up a handful of pins, and continued moving the notices around and affixing each of them securely with four pins.

He watched for a couple of moments, trying to figure out what Scarlett Flynn was about. He'd worked with all kinds of people over the years and prided himself on an ability to be able to work with anyone. He'd often had to work with people who were difficult or shy or different from the norm in some way, but Scarlett was a whole new puzzle for him.

It was a puzzle he knew he'd have to unravel if her time at Silver Arches was going to be at all successful.

11

Security and Discipline

SCARLETT ENTERED the Silver Arches staff entrance and took the stairwell up to the top floor. She was quite used to being reassigned. When she was in school, she was often taken out of one class and put into another. In the army she was frequently moved from one task to another. Intrex had been no different, and now, it appeared, Silver Arches would be the same.

It wasn't lost on her that she was the only person being moved from pillar to post, but she'd long ago discovered it wasn't worth arguing the point.

Before she entered the security office, she paused. She sucked in a quick breath and adjusted her glasses before she walked into the room.

Inside the security office were several banks of occupied desks, and a handful of people looked up at her when she entered the room. She became aware of a strange atmosphere in the room that she couldn't quite put her finger on; however, she thought it centred on her for some reason.

"You must be Scarlett."

She turned to see a short woman walking towards her with her hand outstretched.

"Yes."

"I'm Tara Manning."

Scarlett shook her hand and waited quietly for further orders.

"Come through to my office," Tara instructed.

Scarlett fell into step behind her, taking the offered seat in front of Tara's desk while the older woman closed the door behind them.

"Security is essential to the running of this shopping centre," Tara explained. "We want to ensure a safe environment for everyone, no exception. That means there are rules and they must be obeyed."

Scarlett sat up a little straighter at the strict tone being taken. Tara Manning meant business, and Scarlett appreciated her direct approach and honesty.

Tara took her seat. "There will be a learning curve for you if you want to work in this team. There will be a lot of reading to be done, and then you will shadow one of my senior staff members until you find your feet. It won't be easy, and I need to know if you're prepared to work hard."

Scarlett nodded. "I will do whatever is necessary."

Tara rested her hand on a large box file. "In here are the codes of conduct for Silver Arches, as well as relevant laws, training manuals, staff guides. I need you to read through all of it and take and pass an online test before you are allowed to do certain tasks."

She pushed the box file towards Scarlett, who took the heavy file and placed it on her lap.

"For the first few days, we'll split your time between working with Max and seeing what he does in an average day and working on your paperwork. I'll expect you to get all of that read within a week. Then we'll do the online tests. I'd like for you to pass them within two weeks, which shouldn't be a problem if you've read everything in that box. Does that make sense?"

"Yes."

"Great. I'll show you to your desk, and I'll introduce you to Max. Then he'll give you a tour of the centre." Tara stood.

"I already know my way around the centre," Scarlett explained.

"Not as a member of security. You'll take the tour," Tara told her.

Scarlett stood and followed Tara out of her office. A few moments later, she was being introduced to Max. Unlike the people in facilities, the security team seemed professional and easy to work with. The walls were filled with whiteboards with schedules, business reminders, and security notices rather than questionable calendars and inappropriate quotes printed out from the internet.

Max helped Scarlett log onto the computer and showed her the online tests and then went through the paperwork that related to each test. He told her that they would have an hour in the office before they conducted a tour of the centre and that she could get started on her reading in that time.

Scarlett was pleased to see that Tara maintained a

good level of discipline in the security office. The only sound that could be heard was that of soft typing and the occasional work-related phone call.

Maybe a position in security was just what she needed. Maybe it would be the 'good fit' that people spoke of.

She attempted to keep her expectations down, knowing that she often felt that things were going well only to be later told they had not.

Time would tell if security was right for her.

12

No Time for Lunch

HEATHER TUCKED her folio under her arm and shook the hands of the marketing team from Intrex. As meetings went, it had been fairly painless.

Thankfully, the marketing team were a lot more pleasant to deal with than the financial team or the operations team.

It had been a few weeks since Intrex had become involved with Silver Arches, and they were slowly making their presence known. From a slowdown in recruitment to a rebrand, things were changing.

On the bright side, the Intrex people loved to hold a meeting about every little thing, which meant Heather always had the chance to put forward her point of view and even tweak some of their existing plans.

Heather's role had always included plenty of meetings and discussions, but these days it felt as if she spent more time around large meeting-room tables than she did in the comfort of her own office. If it wasn't for the excellent team she'd surrounded herself with, her usual work stack would have been overflowing by now.

Yasmin had taken the sudden changes in her stride and shown herself to be an excellent gatekeeper, feeding some tasks through to Ravi to share the load. Heather made a mental note to ensure that she appropriately thanked Yasmin for her extra work, probably with some restaurant gift vouchers.

She said farewell to the Intrex marketing team and, instead of heading back to her office, made her way towards the centre. It had been a while since she had performed her usual patrol of the mall.

Not that she was actually *patrolling*, she just enjoyed being in the centre. There was something pleasurable about seeing the stores and the ever-changing shop windows and marketing messaging. The centre felt like a living being that changed through the seasons. It didn't hurt that she occasionally picked up on the odd thing that maintenance needed to turn their attention to. She prided herself on Silver Arches' appearance; it felt like an extension of herself.

Once in the public area, she inhaled deeply and enjoyed the aroma of coffee from the large chain as it mixed with the sweet smell of popcorn from the cart on the lower level.

Shoppers of all sorts bustled through the busy walkway, from the mothers with buggies to the couples gently quarrelling about which wedding gift to get for a friend.

A toddler ran from its parents with impressive speed and made a break for the escalator. Heather detoured and placed a hand on the little one's chest to prevent them from picking up too much speed as a guardian sprinted over.

"Thank you," the woman said.

"No problem." Heather smiled.

The toddler looked up at her and grinned, despite Heather having been the cause of the premature end of its bid for freedom. The woman scooped the child up and went back to the shop.

Heather's stomach growled, and she realised she'd not eaten lunch yet. It was a good opportunity to visit the large food court, which was populated with a large number of both sit-down and quick-service restaurants.

On the way to the food court she took note of a couple of outfits in shop windows that interested her, as well as a pair of boots that would be perfect for DIY projects on her parents' farm.

One of the four entrances to the food court had once been a large and empty space, save for a couple of pieces of art on the walls. Now it had been converted into space for local pop-up shops.

Heather was pleased to see that progress was quickly being made on the individual temporary stores. They weren't much, similar to conference centre stalls, with light and power and enough room for a reasonable amount of stock. She hoped they would give a boost to local retailers and also encourage more of Silver Arches' existing customer base to spend more cash.

"Done with your meeting?" Ravi asked, appearing from inside one of the pop-up shells.

"With the marketing one," Heather confirmed. "I still have one with HR this afternoon."

"Don't forget to eat," Ravi reminded her perceptively.

"I was literally on my way to do just that." She pointed at one of the pop-ups. "Are these lights brighter than the others?"

"They are," Ravi confirmed. "No idea why. We've got an electrician coming out to switch the light fixtures. These units are all meant to be identical."

Heather looked around, noting that the electrical supply came from the wall and trailed along the floor. "Will this be properly covered?"

"Yes, we're getting a raised platform behind all the pop-ups. It will cover all the sins," Ravi explained. "Now, weren't you supposed to be getting yourself some lunch?"

Heather chuckled. She'd already forgotten what she was in the process of doing, too easily distracted by something new and shiny. She knew Ravi could deal with the project and she didn't need to get involved, but she sometimes couldn't help herself.

She held up her hands. "I'm going. I'm going."

As she turned to leave, something caught her eye. She paused and watched as Scarlett Flynn escorted a young teenager through the centre. The young woman had a tight grip on the boy's upper arm, and he appeared to be crying.

Ravi had his hands full, so Heather nodded to him to indicate she'd deal with whatever was happening.

She jogged a little to catch up to the pair. Scarlett had been working in security for two weeks and had settled in well according to Tara. She'd gone through the online tests and certifications required to patrol the centre in half the time of any other security guard.

Heather had hardly heard a word about or from Scarlett in that time and had assumed her issues with the woman were over.

However, seeing Scarlett frogmarch a tearful teenager through the centre made Heather think her problems were just getting started.

"Scarlett?" she called out.

The young woman came to a halt and turned, her grip on the boy still vice-like.

"What's going on?" Heather asked.

Now that she was closer, she could see the boy was very upset. Tears poured down bright, red cheeks and he was shaking.

"He was stealing. I'm taking him to the office and will inform the police."

Heather knew the procedures for dealing with shoplifters, but she also knew that sometimes some lenience was required. Especially when the thief in question was around fourteen years old, well dressed, and absolutely terrified. There was something else going on here; Heather's sixth sense was on heightened alert.

"Please, I didn't mean it," the boy spoke up, his eyes boring into Heather.

"You stole goods valuing thirty-four pounds and eighty-two pence," Scarlett informed him coldly. "I watched you place the items in your bag. You had no intention to pay for them."

Heather realised shoppers were starting to take an interest in what was happening and knew it was time to take the conversation out of the public area.

"Let's take this to the office," Heather suggested. "Let go of his arm."

Scarlett hesitated for a moment, her eyes locking with Heather's questioningly.

"Do it," Heather insisted. "He's not going anywhere. Are you?"

"N-no," the teen stammered.

Scarlett reluctantly let go. She looked to Heather for further guidance.

"Right, let's get this sorted out," Heather suggested, gesturing towards the escalator that would take them to the upper level and the security suite.

13

A Judgement Call

SCARLETT COULDN'T BELIEVE what was happening. She'd successfully apprehended a shoplifter, and now the centre director was making them a cup of tea. The boy, Joshua Buckley, had promptly broken into floods of tears when they had arrived at one of the quiet meeting rooms used to store criminals until the police arrived.

To Scarlett's shock, Heather had put her arm around the boy and led him to an armchair. She'd softly whispered something to him, handed him a handkerchief from her own pocket, and was now making him a hot drink.

Scarlett stood stiffly by the door, unsure what course of action to take.

"So, Joshua, what was it you took?" Heather asked, lifting the just-boiled kettle and pouring hot water into two cups. Scarlett had declined the offer of a beverage.

"He stole a book, a selection of pens, a blank notepad, some novelty erasers, four chocolate bars, a drink—"

Heather held up her hand and Scarlett stopped speaking.

"Is that true?" Heather asked Joshua.

Scarlett couldn't help but let out a sigh. It was a strange questioning technique to ask the offender if they had indeed committed an offence. Scarlett wanted to point that fact out to Heather but considered that Heather must have known that.

At least, she hoped she did. It would be a surprise that she had managed to attain her position if she didn't.

Joshua nodded. "Yes." He wiped at his face again with the white handkerchief.

"Why did you do that?" Heather asked. She picked up the two mugs and placed them on the coffee table before taking a seat in the armchair opposite Joshua.

The boy just shrugged.

"I need to know what's going on if I'm going to help you," Heather told him, her voice soft and gentle.

Scarlett felt more confused than ever. If she'd been left to deal with this, the police would have been on their way to pick the boy up and she'd soon be back at work. Now both she and Heather were spending their valuable time talking to a teenage thief. A thief that didn't seem willing to talk or aware of the amount of costly resources he was sucking up.

"I dunno," Joshua mumbled.

"Drink some tea. I promise you, I make a very good cup of tea," Heather said, picking up her mug. "I don't know about you, but my mother always told me that a cup of tea will solve almost anything."

Joshua grinned ever so slightly. "Yeah, my gran says that." He leaned forward and picked up the other mug.

"Do you live with your gran?" Heather asked.

"No, I live with my dad." He winced as if suddenly remembering something. "He's going to kill me."

"Is it just you and your dad?" Heather fished.

Joshua shook his head. "No, I've got a little brother. Our mum left when he was a little kid. She wasn't right, you know?"

Heather nodded. Scarlett frowned; she had no idea what Joshua was referring to. She wanted to ask in what way his mother wasn't 'right' but refrained; she already felt like an outsider looking in on a private conversation.

"Have you stolen before?" Heather asked. "Not from here, just in general?"

Joshua shook his head. "No. This was the first time; I don't even know why I did it. I don't even need that stuff." He put the mug down on the table and put his head in his hands. "My dad is going to kill me."

Heather lowered her own mug to the table and leaned forward, placing a hand on his knee. "Has your dad been physically violent towards you or your brother?"

Scarlett looked at the huddled mass that was Joshua Buckley. Silence filled the room for a few long moments before the boy slowly nodded, his head still buried in his hands.

Heather stood up and sat down on the arm of Joshua's chair. She laid a hand on his back.

"What are you going to do?" Joshua asked.

"I'm going to let you go with a warning," Heather said.

Scarlett stared at Heather, questioning her with an intense gaze. Heather met Scarlett's look and softly shook her head to indicate that Scarlett should not speak.

"But I want you to do something for me," Heather continued.

Joshua slowly looked up. His cheeks were red and soaked with tears.

"I'm going to give you the number of a free helpline. They help people in your situation. I want you to call them; you don't have to say anything you don't want to, but they are a service for you to call when things get a little much at home. They are completely confidential, so anything you tell them stays between you and them. If you need advice, or help, they can do that for you." Heather ran her hand through Joshua's messy hair to flatten it down. "Will you do that for me?"

He nodded.

"Good. Get your phone out and I'll put the number in for you," Heather said.

He reached into his pocket, unlocked it, and then handed over the device. Heather tapped the details into the phone. "We keep records of what happens here, and we have a lot of CCTV. If we find you stealing again, then we won't be so kind, okay?"

"I know. I'm sorry, I just... I don't even know. I... I wasn't thinking."

Heather handed the phone back. "I know. Just stay out of trouble in the future. Okay?"

Heather instructed Scarlett to wait while she escorted Joshua back to the centre. While she waited, Scarlett took Joshua's half-empty mug to the sink and washed it up and dried it.

All the while she wondered what Heather wanted to

speak to her about. Obviously, she had made some kind of a mistake in her dealing with the shoplifting incident.

Not that she agreed with Heather's way of handling the situation. In fact, Scarlett still felt some residual anger at the centre director for taking control like that. What was the point in having rules and regulations if they could be ignored at any time someone chose? Especially by someone who didn't work in security.

Heather came back into the room. "Take a seat, Scarlett."

Scarlett dried her hands and perched on the edge of the armchair, eager to get the conversation out of the way so she could return to her work.

"Do you understand why I let him go with a warning?" Heather asked.

"No," Scarlett replied honestly. "I think you made an error in judgement."

"Why do you think that?" Heather sat back in her own armchair, casually kicking off her shoes and pulling her legs up under her.

"He committed a crime; he should be punished. Allowing him to leave gives the impression that we don't prosecute, and he will be incentivised to try again."

Heather shrugged a shoulder. "Maybe, but I don't think so. I think this was a special circumstance."

Scarlett resisted the urge to roll her eyes. *Special circumstances* were a mystery to her. Every situation seemed to have them, but she viewed them as a blanket excuse to throw rules out the window.

"I see," Scarlett said.

"Do you?" Heather tilted her head.

Scarlett swallowed. She didn't see, but the response was her go-to for this sort of situation.

"No," she admitted, hating dishonesty.

"I could see in him that he wasn't your usual shoplifter," Heather explained. "I surmised there was something else there."

Scarlett attempted to remain neutral but realised her feelings on the matter must have slipped through when Heather chuckled. She had been told that her facial expressions were a clear window into her soul. Apparently, she just didn't possess the masking skills that everyone else seemed to have.

"I take it you disagree?" Heather asked.

"You cannot be certain that what he told you was the truth. It could have been a fabrication used to get out of situations like this."

"Absolutely, it could have been. I'll admit I've taken a risk. But I feel it's one worth taking. Tell me, how many shoplifters have you encountered since you started working in security?"

"Four," Scarlett replied. "Two when I was shadowing another officer and two on my own. I've also been present at six other discussions with offenders as part of my training."

"And did Joshua look like any of them?"

"I watched him take goods," Scarlett reminded Heather.

"Yes, I know. But did he resemble the others? Were his manner, his clothing, his behaviour the same?"

Scarlett considered that for a moment. Joshua had reacted differently to being caught. He had immediately shown contrition rather than irritation at being discovered. In addition, he was well dressed and didn't seem to have pre-prepared himself to take items. Usually shoplifters would wear ill-fitting clothes in order to hide items on their person. Often they would have a large, empty bag in their possession.

"No," Scarlett allowed.

"And that's one of the reasons I let him go with a warning," Heather explained. "He didn't fit the usual criteria, and I felt there was something else there. I've taken a risk in letting him go, but I'm happy with the decision if I've managed to help put him back on the right path. Sometimes kindness is more important than justice."

Scarlett wasn't so sure, but she didn't want to argue with the boss.

Before she had a chance to reply, there was a knock on the door. It swept open a moment later to reveal Tara.

"Heather, could I have a word?" Tara asked, obviously having seen her through the slim window in the door.

"Yes, we were just finishing up," Heather replied.

Scarlett took the opportunity to stand. "If there is nothing else, I should return to work."

"Sure. Thank you for your efforts," Heather said.

Scarlett wanted to comment that her efforts were in vain if the centre director was going to choose to release every thief she discovered, but she knew that wouldn't go down well. Instead she made her escape from the room, nodding at Tara as she left.

14

Clap Them in Irons

HEATHER WATCHED Scarlett leave and let out a small sigh. She wasn't sure if she'd managed to get through to the young woman or not.

Tara entered the room and closed the door behind her. She took Scarlett's vacated seat.

"Sorry to interrupt. I wanted to quickly talk to you, but it wasn't worth setting up a formal meeting," Tara explained.

This was one of the reasons why Heather liked Tara; she had an excellent sense for what could be solved during a five-minute discussion and what couldn't.

"No problem. What's up?"

"She just left the room," Tara quipped.

Heather felt her body sag. "Oh? I thought things were going well."

"They are, and they are not," Tara said. "On one hand, she's great. One of the best officers I've had, to be honest. She's dedicated, observant, and she knows the rulebook back to front."

"I'm sensing a but?" Heather asked.

"But she's creating issues within the team."

Heather wasn't exactly surprised by that news. Working with others didn't seem to be one of Scarlett's strengths. She raised her eyebrow to encourage Tara to continue.

"She's started ratting on team members when they arrive for their shift a minute or two late. If she sees someone commit what she calls an 'infraction,' she writes it up in an official report and gives it to me."

Heather couldn't help but snigger. She covered her mouth with her hand. "Okay, so she's a little keen on the rules?"

"You could say that, but the problem is, people know what she's doing. She's not quiet about it. In fact, she told Dominic that she was going to write him up."

"What had he done?"

"Wrong shoes. Not in the uniform rules. He'd got a new pair and they'd given him a blister. Long, boring story, but the point is that he had a valid reason and she wrote him up anyway. Not that she should be snitching on her fellow team members at all."

Heather rubbed at her forehead, feeling the beginning of a headache. "Okay, I'm assuming that you've already tried to talk to her?"

"I have, and she's agreed to limit her report writing to the more serious infractions. But that's not the main issue. The problem is that she's created a rift between her and the rest of the team. More so, the rest of the team are becoming unified *against* her."

"Ah." Heather understood now. If any team needed to

work as one cohesive group, it was security. A lone wolf wouldn't get far in that department.

"I'm not giving up yet," Tara said. She seemed to bristle a little at the thought that she might ever do so. "But I wanted to make you aware of what is happening. She's a great asset; I want to keep her. But if she can't be a team player, then she may have to go."

"I understand."

"I can ask her to stop writing reports, but I can't make her integrate if she doesn't want to. She eats lunch in the food court every day rather than eat with the team in our breakroom. Little things like that are setting her apart from the rest of the department."

Heather could imagine the problem, especially considering that Silver Arches was such a close-knit team. She herself often spoke about all staff being a family of sorts.

Now it seemed a member of that family didn't want to play with the others. In fact, it sounded like that person didn't want to engage with anyone else at all.

And Heather could absolutely see that, having spoken to Scarlett a couple of times.

The problem was that Heather didn't know why Scarlett was the way she was. Yes, there was the fact that she had been nicknamed the Robot by her previous colleagues, but where had that come from? Was it simply a part of Scarlett's personality, or was there a reason for her reluctance to integrate? Did she feel above everyone else? Was she shy?

Heather had no idea, but it looked like she would need to find out.

"Thank you for bringing this to my attention," she said.

"Keep trying to bring her into the fold. I'll see if I can have a word with her too."

"I'll do my best," Tara said. "May I ask why you were both in here?"

"Troubled teenager caught shoplifting," Heather explained. "Scarlett wasn't pleased with me letting him go with just a warning."

Tara laughed. "No, Scarlett is more the 'clap them in irons' type."

"So I discovered! I tried to highlight to her what I had seen in him, but I don't know if I got through to her."

Tara smiled knowingly. "Yes, I have that same issue with her at times. I don't know if I'm making my point understood or not. Time will tell, I suppose."

"It certainly will."

Tara stood up, saying she had to get back to work. Once she had left, Heather leaned back into the comfortable armchair and considered the Scarlett conundrum.

It wasn't long before her stomach rumbled and she remembered that she had, once again, forgotten to eat lunch. Glancing at her watch, she realised she had just enough time to grab a bite to eat before her next meeting.

15

Setting Up Shop

RAVI LOWERED the three heavy boxes to the ground and let out a pained grunt.

"Surely, that must be all of them?" he asked hopefully.

Nico was standing on a chair, adjusting some of the spotlights in her new pop-up. She turned and looked over her shoulder, evaluating the boxes.

"For now," she said.

Ravi couldn't believe how many books, stickers, post-cards, calendars, and more Nico thought she was going to sell in her first week in Silver Arches. He admired her confidence.

Nico's assistant had dropped out at the last minute, and so Ravi stepped in to help Nico with the set-up. He'd expected to spend his lunchtime putting up signage and setting up the till, but Nico had other ideas, ideas that lived in heavy boxes she'd left in her car.

"You're out of shape," she told him before returning to angling the lighting rig. "Panting like an old man."

"Books are heavy," he complained.

"Are they?" Nico asked innocently.

"This is a health and safety violation," a new voice spoke up.

Ravi walked around to the front of the temporary store to see Scarlett Flynn standing in front of a loose cable with a displeased look on her face. The cable had been draped on the floor for less than two minutes and was obviously a part of the work they were currently doing.

"We know, we're changing the lights out. It will be fixed in a few moments," Ravi explained.

Scarlett looked at him with uncertainty. "I can't leave a health and safety violation unattended."

Ravi wanted to roll his eyes. Of course Scarlett would want to be by the book about the cable, the cable that was most definitely not a trip hazard and not in anyone's way.

But it did *technically* represent a hazard, and so Ravi knew he had to clear it up immediately.

"I'll… do it now." He went over to the cable, realising it was attached to a mass of other cables, and started to unthread them.

"Do you read much?" Nico asked Scarlett.

Scarlett turned to look at Nico. "No."

"You like stickers?" Nico held up a sheet of stickers emblazoned with rainbows.

"No."

"Postcards?" Nico gestured to a stack of postcards.

"No."

Nico smiled, completely unfazed. "What do you like?"

Ravi paused and watched Scarlett with interest. The young woman seemed to put thought into the question, but after a few silent moments she simply shrugged her shoulder.

"I don't know."

Ravi felt his eyes widen. Did Scarlett genuinely not know what she was interested in, or did she just say that to stop Nico asking her questions? He couldn't imagine the former. Who didn't know what they liked?

"Never mind," Nico said brightly. "Keep looking and you'll find it."

Scarlett didn't seem to have a reply to that.

Nico got her phone out of her back pocket. "I'm trying to add more photos to my Instagram account. Can I have a selfie with you as my first almost-customer?"

Scarlett looked uncomfortable. "I'm not a customer. You're not even open."

"Almost-customer," Nico corrected.

"There's no such thing," Scarlett replied.

"There is. Anyway, I'll make it very clear that you simply stopped by to report my health and safety violation," Nico told her. "I'm Nico, by the way."

"Scarlett."

"Nice to meet you, Scarlett. So, what do you say? Selfie?" Nico waved her phone a little. "It will pass the time while we wait for Ravi to clear up our mess. And it will help my Instagram account."

"Very well," Scarlett said.

Nico exited the pop-up and positioned Scarlett in front of the store; she then stood beside her and held up the phone to check the view.

"Thanks for doing this. I need to get into the habit of

asking more people," Nico said. "Apparently we need to document our lives through photos these days."

"You're welcome," Scarlett said, though she sounded uncertain.

Nico held up the phone. "Right then, smile!"

"Why?"

"To show that you're happy," Nico said.

"I'm not," Scarlett replied seriously.

Nico burst out laughing. "Okay, fair enough. Don't smile; I'll smile enough for both of us."

Ravi cleared away the cables just as Nico released Scarlett from her social media duties. Scarlett looked at the area and gave him an approving nod.

"All done," Ravi said, not missing the irony that Scarlett was about twelve pay grades below him and still happily telling him what to do and when.

"Agreed." Scarlett spun on her heel to leave. Then she stopped, turned, and looked intently at Ravi for a second. "Thank you," she added.

Ravi blinked in surprise. Before he had a chance to reply, Scarlett had turned again and continued her patrol.

"Who was that?" Nico asked. "She's fascinating."

"That is Leo Flynn's daughter," Ravi explained.

"Where do I know that name?" Nico asked, cocking her head to the side.

"He is the big boss at Intrex, the investment company."

Nico's eyes widened and her mouth formed a small *o*. She turned to look at Scarlett's retreating form and then back to Ravi.

"Why's she in a security uniform?"

"Because she works in security now," Ravi said. "Leo

asked Heather to find a role for her. He thinks she's diffi-cult. And, well, she is a bit, to be fair to the man."

"She's hilarious," Nico said, though not without kind-ness. "And fascinating."

"She's certainly an interesting one," Ravi allowed. "Not made many friends, though. People have started calling her the Robot; it's what the people at Intrex used to call her."

"That's shitty," Nico said.

"It is, but she doesn't exactly endear herself to people. As you could see."

"Still, it must be hard to have no friends at work," Nico added.

"I've tried to get her involved in things," Ravi said, "but she just doesn't want to join in anything. I do keep trying, though."

Nico bumped his shoulder with her own. "Good. Don't give up. Not everyone can be average and boring; sometimes people are weird and wonderful. We need to keep them that way."

Ravi smiled at her. He loved the fresh way that Nico saw things. Different wasn't scary or wrong; it was some-thing to be embraced.

Nico collected people and had more friends than anyone else he knew. If you wanted to source an artist, a painter, a builder, a plumber, a pilot for a fixed-wing two-seater plane, Nico knew someone. Nico knew everyone. And what's more, Nico knew how to connect with every-one. She had an ability to read people like a barcode and adapt herself to them.

Ravi made a decision to redouble his efforts to try to

integrate Scarlett into the Silver Arches family. It had played on his mind that the woman was still such an outsider. It had been quite a few weeks since she joined the team, and she was still regarded as odd and robotic by the staff.

Ravi just didn't know how to change things. Especially considering that Scarlett seemed perfectly satisfied with the way things were.

16

Prefer to Be Alone

HEATHER ENTERED the upper level of the food court. She looked over the railing and gazed down at the lower level.

She hadn't believed Tara when she said that Scarlett ate at the same table, at the same time, every single day, but sure enough, there she was. Heather smiled to herself; creature of habit didn't even begin to describe Scarlett.

Tara had contacted Heather a second time after their brief conversation in one of the security meeting rooms.

She'd asked Heather to please try to have a word with Scarlett and attempt to bring her back to the flock. Or at least get a little closer to the flock so she wasn't so universally disliked.

Heather had a reputation for being able to get through to people. She didn't know if she'd have much luck with Scarlett, but she was willing to try.

She crossed the food court and took the escalator downstairs, wondering how she'd approach Scarlett. Was it better to pretend she was passing, or to make it clear that it was a planned visit?

She decided on the latter. Scarlett didn't seem to be one for subterfuge, and so Heather decided to take her lead on things.

Heather approached the table, where it was located in the far corner of the dining area. Scarlett was eating a pre-packaged sandwich she had picked up from a nearby chain. On the table were a bottle of water, a napkin, and Scarlett's phone. All seemed perfectly positioned rather than randomly put down on the table.

"Afternoon," Heather greeted her.

Scarlett looked up in surprise. She looked around, almost as if she expected Heather to be greeting someone else. Heather stood her ground and waited for Scarlett to settle down and reply.

"Hello."

Heather smiled and pulled out the other chair at the table, seating herself opposite Scarlett. The younger woman looked displeased at the unexpected company, but Heather knew she couldn't let that discourage her. She had to speak with Scarlett and try to resolve the various issues that had come up.

"I see you're sitting alone," Heather began.

"I was."

Heather smiled. Scarlett's comment wasn't necessarily rude, but it could certainly be considered as such by some. She suspected this was some of the problem.

"I hear that you always eat here rather than in the security breakroom?" Heather continued.

"I prefer to be alone," Scarlett replied, putting her sandwich down and putting her phone to sleep.

"That must make it hard to make friends," Heather enquired.

"There is no one to make friends with," Scarlett said.

"We employ hundreds of people. There must be someone you want to be friends with," Heather said.

Scarlett tilted her head to the side slightly, pinning Heather with a questioning gaze. "Am I required to make friends at work?"

Heather hesitated. Of course it wasn't a requirement, and such a thing could never be regulated anyway. It was just the done thing for most people. But not Scarlett Flynn, it seemed.

"Don't you feel lonely?" Heather asked.

Scarlett seemed to give that serious consideration.

"Sometimes. But not often."

Heather couldn't really argue with that, and she couldn't order Scarlett to socialise with people if she didn't want to. She wondered if she could appeal to her better nature.

"Many of us feel that the staff at Silver Arches is more like a family than a collection of employees. We socialise together, we're there for each other. Some people consider their work colleagues to also be their best friends. You know, we've even had some marriages between staff members."

Scarlett just stared at Heather as if she were waiting for an actual point to be made.

"I'm just saying that maybe, if you tried to befriend some of your work colleagues, you might be surprised where that would lead."

"To marriage?" Scarlett asked, surprise obvious in her tone.

Heather smiled. "Well, maybe. Maybe not."

"I prefer to be alone. Am I expected to socialise with people who do not like me?" Scarlett asked.

"Not expected, no. But maybe people would like you if you spent more time with them?"

"Unlikely," Scarlet said matter-of-factly.

Heather laughed and leaned back in her chair. "Why do you say that?"

Scarlett regarded her. "Experience."

"Not experience of *these* people." Heather wouldn't allow her staff to be written off so quickly.

"No," Scarlett allowed. "But general experience indicates that I am... an acquired taste."

"Maybe give them the opportunity to ta... to get to know you?"

"I prefer to be alone, but even if that were not the case, I'm aware that minds have been made up and I am disliked. Unless you are ordering me to make friends?"

Heather shook her head. "No, I couldn't and wouldn't order you to do that. I just wanted you to integrate with your teammates; I think it would be a positive thing for you."

Scarlett considered that statement for a full five seconds before she picked up her sandwich again. "I disagree."

Heather chuckled. "Okay. How about we make a deal: I'll not pressure you into making friends with people if you ease up on reporting on your colleagues?"

Scarlett's eyes widened in mild surprise. "You don't

wish for me to advise management when an employee is in breach of regulation?"

"Depends on the breach." Heather leaned forward, placing her interlaced hands on the table. "Reporting people when they are two minutes late to their shift isn't essential, but it will upset your teammates."

Scarlett considered this. "I see. You would like me to not report timekeeping violations?"

"That's a start."

An eyebrow raised. "There's more?"

"I think it would be advisable for you to not report on anything your colleagues do unless it's an incredibly serious breach. Like theft. Or murder."

Scarlett looked intently at Heather's grinning face.

"You're being facetious," she finally decided.

"I am. A little." Heather couldn't help but smile. Scarlett was so unique and, in some ways, quite pure and innocent. She seemed to completely lack social skills, and while many people would find that off-putting and difficult to deal with, Heather found it fascinating. Scarlett was a puzzle to be solved, like the multitude of puzzle books that she collected at home but far more interesting.

"Why do you report your colleagues? Don't you realise that would upset them?" Heather asked.

"They are breaking the terms of their employment. It's wrong." Scarlett took a small bite of her sandwich.

"Do you report it because of your father?" Heather had to know if Leo was a component in all of this, though she doubted it.

Scarlett shook her head. "My father and I don't speak."

"You must speak at some point."

"Very rarely. He doesn't like me."

"I'm sure that's not true," Heather said.

"It is true," Scarlet declared. "It doesn't make me sad."

Heather didn't know how to respond to that. She'd be devastated if she didn't have a good relationship with her parents. She knew not everyone was that lucky. Some people, through no fault of their own, had terrible parents and had no choice but to cut them out of their lives.

But Leo seemed to care for Scarlett on some level. He called her difficult but still wanted her safely employed; that indicated some level of care to Heather.

"Are you enjoying working in the security department?" Heather asked, trying to move the subject on to something less dire.

"It is interesting," Scarlett allowed.

Heather waited for Scarlett to elaborate, but nothing came.

"Just… interesting?" Heather fished.

"Yes." Scarlett looked at her passively, seemingly not noticing Heather's exasperation at needing to pull everything from her. Or maybe pretending not to notice. Heather hadn't decided yet.

"Am I to be reassigned?" Scarlett asked.

"Do you want to be?" Heather replied.

Scarlett shook her head. "No."

"Well, there you go then. A ringing endorsement." Heather smiled. "Has anyone ever told you that you can be a little difficult to speak to?"

"Frequently." Scarlett took another bite of her sandwich.

Heather chuckled. *Does she like acting out like this?*

Heather wondered. *Is it a part of her personality? Or is she messing with us all?*

"Well, I enjoyed our chat. Thank you, Scarlett." Heather stood up and tucked her chair back under the table.

Scarlett looked up at her in disbelief. "You did?"

"I did. Have a nice lunch. I hope we see each other again soon."

Heather walked through the food court and back towards her office. She still didn't really know what to make of Scarlett other than that she was fascinating.

It was rare that Heather struggled to get an understanding of someone, but that was definitely the case with the young security officer. Heather just couldn't work her out, and that was rather exhilarating.

17

Book Loan Buddy

Scarlett stared sternly at the young man through the store window. He swallowed hard. She slowly raised an eyebrow. He stopped sliding the bottle of hair product up his sleeve and instead put it into the shopping basket in his other hand.

She nodded to him and then continued her patrol.

Tara had recently discussed the merits of simply being seen over performing an immediate arrest of a suspect. Scarlett had bristled at the idea at first. It felt like allowing potential criminals to get away with their almost-crimes.

She had slowly come around to Tara's way of thinking. While the nearly-perpetrators didn't get escorted from the premises, Scarlett could amuse herself by frightening them with a single look.

It was also far more efficient. Rather than using the time to take an individual off the shop floor and deal with them in a one-on-one scenario that could take up to an hour, she had the opportunity to prevent multiple crimes taking place.

Often with a simple look.

Scarlett didn't like the injustice of letting people go, but she could appreciate the value in the time saved.

"Scarlett!"

She looked up to see Nico waving her over. The new pop-up shops were now up and running and had been for a few days. They provided a new set of problems for security as their stalls were open to the elements and therefore provided an easier target for opportunistic thieves.

Scarlett marched over to Nico, wondering what crime had been committed.

"Yes?" she asked, looking at the selection of products to see what may have been stolen.

"How are you?" Nico asked cheerfully as she adjusted some postcards on a rotating stand.

"How am I?"

"Yes. You're one of four people I know here, and I wanted a chat. How are you?"

"I'm working," Scarlett replied.

"Figured out any interests yet?" Nico asked. "We decided you didn't like books, stickers, or postcards. How about... music?"

Scarlett opened and then closed her mouth. She considered the question; music wasn't displeasing. Unless it was too loud, in which case it was irritating. Or too quiet and therefore a distraction. She wouldn't consider it an interest as such, but it also wasn't something she necessarily disliked.

"I'm indifferent to music," she eventually answered.

"Okay, then television? What have you been watching

lately?" Nico moved on to the next subject without any hesitation.

"I don't own a television." She adjusted her glasses a little.

"Me neither. I watch everything through my tablet these days. So, what have you been watching?"

"I don't watch television shows," Scarlett stated.

"How about comics?" Nico asked.

Scarlett glanced to the comics in the pop-up. She shook her head. "I'm sorry," she said. "I don't have any interests."

"You do, you just haven't found them yet," Nico told her. She leaned on the counter and regarded Scarlett with a smile. "A few years ago, I decided I wanted to try drawing. I went out and got some fancy pencils and some high-grade paper, and I sketched. It was fun."

Nico stood up and stretched her back out. "Of course, I was bloody terrible at it and quickly lost interest in the whole thing. But I was interested in it for a while."

Scarlett considered sketching. She'd always been competent at recreating what she saw around her on paper, but the act had never served a purpose and so it quickly bored her.

Nico held up a book. "I read this last night. It's brilliant. I bet you'd like it."

Scarlett wondered how Nico could possibly make such a bold claim considering she hardly knew her. Especially considering that Scarlett had already confessed to not being interested in reading.

"Here." Nico held the book towards Scarlett. "You can have it."

Scarlett shook her head. "As a member of The Arches Group, I'm not allowed to accept gifts from stores."

Nico smiled. "Okay, fine, *borrow* this and give it back to me when you've read it. Seriously, I think you'd like it. I thought it was fab."

Scarlett considered that this was a simple fudging of the rules, and she wasn't sure she liked the sound of that.

Could the loan of a book still be considered a gift? Probably by some. But Nico was being kind and Scarlett didn't want to be rude. As one of the few people who truly followed the rules, Scarlett decided that maybe this was a time where she could bend them a little.

"Very well." She held out her hand.

Nico handed over the book. "I should probably mention it's a lesbian romance. You'd be surprised how many people are shocked that I sell books with same-sex relationships in them. As if all these rainbows hanging up weren't a clue. Are you okay with that?"

"The rainbows?"

"No, the fact it's a lesbian romance."

Scarlett shrugged. "I have been in relationships with men and women, so it's of little matter to me."

Suddenly, Steph's face flashed up in Scarlett's mind. It had been a long time since she'd thought of her ex-girlfriend.

Not surprising, as it had been practically another lifetime ago. Back when she was in the army and thought she had a purpose in life.

"I'm not good with relationships, but I will read the book," Scarlett added. "And then I will return it, as per our loan agreement."

Nico gave a sloppy salute. "Absolutely, book loan buddy. Hope you enjoy it!"

Scarlett wasn't sure how to respond to the salute or the comment. So she didn't.

18

Wake-Up Call

HEATHER GROANED.

She'd never been good with mornings. While some people seemed to wake from sleep in the time it took to snap fingers, Heather had always struggled with waking up.

And even when she was finally awake, it took a while for her to properly function. She always set her alarm an hour earlier than it needed to be so that she had plenty of time to get herself together and figure out which way was up and what day of the week it was.

Which was why it took her a while to realise that something was different this particular morning.

It wasn't the soft and pleasant tone of her morning alarm that was waking her up. It was the repetitive, insistent, and growing-ever-louder tone of her phone ringing with an incoming call.

She sat up and crawled across the bed to snatch up her mobile from where it rumbled on the bedside table. She looked at the screen bleary-eyed for a moment before things came into focus.

The first thing she noticed was that Tara Manning was calling her. The second thing was that it was almost three in the morning.

Having her security manager call her at any time outside of office hours was never likely to be a good sign, but the call in the middle of the night was enough to cause Heather's stomach to somersault.

"Tara?" she answered, trying to sound more awake than she felt.

"Sorry for waking you," Tara said. "I've had a call from the police. There's been a break-in at Silver Arches. I'm in Scotland, but they have contacted the on-duty keyholder."

Heather sat up and rubbed at her eyes. She had a vague memory of Tara requesting leave to go on a short romantic getaway to the Highlands. Which meant that Heather was the next senior member of staff to attend a break-in.

A shopping mall as big as Silver Arches had several keyholders for such emergency situations. Someone would have been woken up the moment any alarms were tripped at the centre and they would have been asked to meet the police.

If the matter was deemed serious, a senior member of the team would be asked to attend.

"I logged into the CCTV system, and it looks pretty bad at the south entrance. I think they attempted to drive a car through the doors," Tara explained.

Heather felt her eyebrows raise. "Bold."

"Messy," Tara corrected.

Heather got out of bed and fumbled for the light switch. It wasn't the first time that Silver Arches had been broken into, and it probably wouldn't be the last. But that didn't mean Heather had got any better at being woken in the middle of the night to deal with it.

"Okay, I'm on my way in," Heather said. "You get back to bed and try to enjoy your holiday."

"I'll try. I'm in the doghouse," Tara replied. "Some people don't understand that the police have my phone number regardless of whether I'm on holiday or not."

Heather chuckled. It looked like there was a bright side to being alone.

"Good luck," she said as she signed off. She opened her wardrobe and grabbed some clothes.

It wasn't strictly necessary for her to be the one onsite when something happened; she could have long ago delegated these duties to someone else, but Heather liked to lead from the front.

She would never hand a job to a member of staff that she wasn't prepared to do herself, and so her name remained on the senior keyholder roster and now and then a call came in on her day off or in the middle of the night. It was all part of the job.

As she stripped off her pyjamas and pulled on some jeans and a thick roll neck, she tried to think who was on duty that evening. Someone had been awoken by the initial alarm going off, and depending on who that was, they might have reached the scene before the police did.

She supposed she'd find out shortly.

The streets were empty, which meant that Heather managed to get to the centre in record-breaking time without once going over the speed limit.

Of course she was keen to get there as soon as possible, but she didn't want to run the risk of getting caught by the multiple speed cameras that lined the busy roads surrounding the centre.

When she was within sight of the centre, she didn't need to guess where the attempted break-in had taken place. The entire area was covered in flashing blue lights. As she pulled into the large car park and got closer to the scene, she saw two ambulances, five police cars, and even a police van.

A police officer waved her down, and she opened the car window.

"I'm Heather Bailey, centre director," she greeted him, holding up her work ID pass for him to look at.

He took the pass and examined it for a beat before nodding and handing it back. He pointed to the cluster of cars.

"You'll want to speak to DI Armstrong; he's in charge."

She thanked him and drove towards the scene of the crime. By the centre doors she could see a small, crumpled car and piles of shattered glass. It seemed that the driver had managed to destroy the first set of doors but had stalled before getting to the second set.

While they hadn't been successful in breaking in, they had managed to cause a lot of damage.

She got out of her car and sucked in a deep breath of crisp morning air. It was going to be a long day.

She walked towards the person she assumed was DI

Armstrong, and she glanced towards the open door of one of the ambulances to see two teenage boys being treated for what looked like superficial facial wounds, police officers watching over them.

Heather shook her head. It would be teenage boys. She didn't like to profile people, but she couldn't remember a time when it hadn't been teenage boys.

As she passed the second ambulance, she glanced up and expected to see more of the same. She stopped dead when she saw the paramedic holding a compress to the forehead of someone she instantly recognised.

"Scarlett?" Heather asked.

Scarlett looked up.

Heather gasped. There were minor cuts and contusions all over her face. Blood ran down her face to trickle onto her white, long-sleeve T-shirt; more blood matted her normally white-blonde hair.

"What happened?" Heather stepped closer, still in some shock at seeing Scarlett so beaten up.

"I received a call at two twenty-nine from the alarm company," Scarlett explained calmly. "I arrived on scene at two forty-two to see a car attempting to gain access to the centre."

"She literally stood between the car and the centre," the paramedic explained, a sigh coming soon after. "Someone thinks she's invincible."

Heather blinked. "You... stood in front of the car?"

"I made a tactical calculation that they wouldn't attempt to use the car as a battering ram if I was in front of it," Scarlett said.

"And?" Heather demanded.

"I was wrong," Scarlett said simply.

"They drove at you?" Heather felt the breath leave her lungs. She looked at the paramedic. "They drove at her?"

"Apparently so," he replied. "She's got good reflexes, though; she jumped out of the way."

"Into broken glass," Scarlett explained. She held up her hands, which were bandaged.

Heather pinched the bridge of her nose. She'd rather the centre was robbed than a member of her team be injured. Why couldn't Scarlett see that? Why put herself in extreme danger?

"I believe these are yours, Miss Flynn."

Heather turned to see a police officer approaching, holding out a pair of broken glasses—Scarlett's glasses. They were useless now, nothing more than scratched frames with shattered lenses. He placed them on an empty shelf in the ambulance and looked at Heather.

"I'm Detective Inspector Armstrong," he introduced himself.

"Heather Bailey, centre director."

"Ah, excellent. I'm just getting some final details from one of my officers, and then I'll be able to brief you on the situation."

Heather nodded. "I'd like to talk to my security officer first."

"Of course. Come and find me when you're ready," Armstrong said before moving away and talking to some of his officers.

Heather turned back to look at Scarlett. It was shocking to see the usually immaculate woman in such a state of disarray.

"Are you okay?" she asked.

Scarlett didn't reply. Instead she looked toward the paramedic as if she wanted him to answer the question.

He took it in his stride and replied, "Mainly cuts and bruises. Looks worse than it is, but she needs to be told no more heroics."

"She will be told just that," Heather promised, giving Scarlett a soft glare for good measure.

Scarlett just looked back at her, calm and unfazed by the whole thing.

"We'll talk when you're feeling better," Heather promised. "Shall I call your father?"

"No, he is very busy," Scarlett said.

"I'm sure he'll want to hear what's happened and will be relieved to know that you're okay," Heather insisted.

"He's unaware of my involvement."

"But he should know. He's your father."

"He wouldn't be interested," Scarlett said with a cold certainty that stopped Heather from arguing the point any further.

Heather swallowed down any argument she might have had and simply nodded.

"Very well. If he asks, I'll have to tell him," Heather said. "And he will ask, because I intend to investigate the possibility of suing them for attempted manslaughter."

"I stood in front of the car," Scarlett reminded her.

"And they chose to drive it at you," Heather argued. "Anyway, I'm not going to get into this now. Follow the paramedic's instructions."

Scarlett simply inclined her head, indicating that she agreed and that the conversation was over.

Heather stepped away from the ambulance, not knowing what do or say or how to offer comfort to someone who seemed to not want any.

She just couldn't fathom Scarlett's actions. Who put themselves in front of a car to protect a building? Why would Scarlett do such a thing when she seemed to have little care for the company or her co-workers? And why would she believe that her father wouldn't care about her injuries?

Heather shook her head and tried to focus on other things, like getting the centre in a state where it could be open for business in a few short hours. She pulled her phone out of her coat pocket and started to call her team.

19

Not Informed

RAVI SMOTHERED a yawn behind his hand and shivered a little at the cold morning air that whipped around him. Thankfully the sun was now rising, and he knew the crispness would soon give way to warmer temperatures.

The shattered glass had been cleaned away, and the emergency glaziers were working hard to get the large panels for the doors replaced. Ravi watched over them while also keeping members of the public away and directing them to the several other entrances available.

Some people did as they were told, and some wanted to hang around and see what had happened. Ravi didn't mind that so much, as long as they stayed behind his temporary tape barrier that fluttered a little in the wind.

One thing that never ceased to amuse Ravi was the amount of people who seemed completely oblivious to their surroundings. At least three times in the last hour he had called out to people who had ducked under the emergency tape in order to enter the centre. Some people were just in a world of their own and didn't seem to notice the police car, glaziers, abandoned car, and more.

"Excuse me, sir!" Ravi called to an older gentleman who was walking straight for the door. "You'll have to use the other entrance, up by John Lewis!"

The man stopped and looked at Ravi as if he'd said something utterly ridiculous.

"This entrance is being repaired," Ravi explained, smiling warmly at the elderly man.

The man looked around and blinked a couple of times, as if only now seeing the hive of activity. He nodded to Ravi and turned and left the area.

Ravi shook his head and grinned. People were such strange creatures sometimes.

His phone rang, still in his hand from the multiple calls he'd had with various people throughout the morning. He saw Tara Manning's name flash up and smiled.

"Hey, sleepyhead!" he greeted her with a chuckle.

"I was one of the first people called; I've already had my early-morning wake-up," she told him. "How is everything? Should I come back? I can get the nine-ten train and be there—"

"No need," Ravi said quickly. "Everything's under control."

"Are you sure? I feel like I should be there. What abo—"

"Tara, have a holiday. Seriously, we're fine. Everything went to plan and we're fine. Don't worry."

He heard her sigh over the phone. "Okay, look, in my office in the top drawer is the schedule for today. You're going to need to move—"

"Already have. Stuart is taking over for Scarlett's morning shift. We're on top of everything."

"How is Scarlett? I texted her, but I didn't get a reply. Well, I did, but no actual information about how she was. More an official report on what happened."

Ravi thought back to when Heather had told him of the situation she'd encountered when she had arrived first thing. She'd seemed more shaken by Scarlett's appearance and her refusal to acknowledge her injuries than she had by the gaping hole in the door of her beloved Silver Arches.

"She was injured, but just superficial cuts and bruises," Ravi explained, glossing over the facts. Tara was tough, but she had a heart of gold and would feel guilty to know that a member of her team had been injured. Moreover, he was positive that she'd kill Scarlett for being so reckless with her own life.

He noticed someone else approaching his cordon and looked up to tell them to stay back but stopped when he realised it was Leo Flynn.

"Gotta go, Tara; the big boss is here. Enjoy your holiday, that's an order," Ravi said before hanging up the call.

He quickly unclipped the radio from his belt and tuned it to the channel he used to communicate directly with Heather.

"The eagle has landed," he said.

It was a silly code, designed to make Heather roll her eyes and mutter at how ridiculous he was, but Ravi knew that Heather had lingering concerns about Leo's presence and the effect he would have on Silver Arches. Anything he could do to lighten the mood was a bonus in these unsettled times.

Leo spotted Ravi and headed over to him.

"Morning, sir," Ravi greeted him politely.

"Morning," Leo grumbled. "What's the situation?"

Ravi was used to acts of vandalism but suspected that Leo wasn't. He cast his mind back to the first few times he had seen someone spray graffiti or run their car into a wall in Silver Arches. It had been infuriating, almost heart-breaking. Nowadays it was a part of the job. Entitled youths took frequent potshots at what they viewed to be an easy target.

"The centre is open for business as usual. We've sealed off this door from the inside and out. All glass and other hazardous materials are cleared away; the glaziers will be finished within a couple of hours, and then we'll be able to open this door again." Ravi gestured to the car the vandals had used. "The police are finishing up taking evidence from the vehicle, and it will be towed away by lunchtime."

"And the gits that did this?" Leo asked, anger sparking in his eyes.

"Arrested and awaiting prosecution," Heather said from behind them.

Ravi realised she must have been nearby when he radioed her.

Leo looked at Heather, a little anger in his eyes. "And when was I going to be informed about this? I heard about all this on the news!"

Heather stood her ground. "Would you like to be

advised of every incident? We suffer an attempted break-in of some description once or twice a month. I can call you when I'm summoned if you wish? Obviously, these incidents often happen in the middle of the night. This one was at three in the morning, but if you want to be kept advised, then I can include a call to you in our official procedures?"

Ravi was glad Leo wasn't facing him as he couldn't contain his smirk. Heather's tone was calm and even, not rude but not taking any nonsense from Leo either.

"I would have thought this kind of thing would be well below your pay grade," Heather said, indicating the glaziers who were currently heaving an enormous glass panel into place.

There was a tense moment where Ravi thought it could go either way. Leo could either be angry at Heather's tone and insinuation, or he could...

"Okay, okay, you win," Leo said, a chuckle immediately following his words.

Ravi let out a small sigh. Thankfully, Heather's gamble had paid off. It was one of the things he admired most about Heather, her ability to read people and situations and react accordingly.

"So, this is a frequent thing?" Leo asked.

"Sadly, yes. We have every measure in place to stop them from penetrating the centre, but we are a target. We need to have easy access for customers, especially at busy times. With deliveries and staff working throughout the night on displays and such, we can't completely shut down the car parks," Heather explained. "But we do catch and prosecute. Very, very few people have ever gotten past any of the main doors and into the actual centre. And once they are in, there's nothing for them as each individual store has its own shutters and security in place."

"We find it's more for vandalism than theft," Ravi added.

"Exactly," Heather agreed. "We're well insured, and we always prosecute."

Leo sucked in a big breath and slowly let it out again. After a moment of contemplation, he nodded. "I see. Right, well, I can see this is in good hands."

"Actually," Heather said, her tongue darting out to lick her lips before she spoke. "It was Scarlett who arrived first on scene and stopped the vandals. You would have been very proud, I'm sure."

Leo barely reacted to that news. "Good, good," he muttered, his eyes still on the glaziers.

"She was injured, but the paramedic said it was mainly cuts and bruises. She'll be back at work in no time, but I gave her a couple of days off to recuperate. So, she'll be at home if you want to check in on her," Heather suggested.

"I'll drop her an email," Leo replied casually. "What are you doing this Saturday?"

Heather blinked. "Me?"

"You," he confirmed.

"Working here until four," she replied.

"My wife is having a birthday party Saturday evening. Starts at seven," Leo said.

"Okay?" Heather looked as confused as Ravi felt.

"You're invited." He turned to Ravi. "You are as well."

Ravi held his hands up. "I would love to, but unfortunately I have the night shift here. But Heather will happily represent us both, I'm certain."

Heather glared at him briefly before smiling at Leo. "I'd be delighted. Should I bring anything?"

"Just yourself," Leo said. "I'll email you the details."

"I look forward to it." Heather sucked in a quick breath. "I really do think that Scarlett would appreciate a visit from you. As I say, she was rather bruised from the—"

"I have to go," Leo said, looking at his watch. "Well done dealing with all of this. It's good to know that I have the right team in place."

He patted them both on the shoulder and turned to leave. "See you Saturday," he said as he left.

Heather slowly shook her head. "How can he not care about her? She's his daughter."

"Maybe there's history there you don't know about?" Ravi suggested.

"Still, he is her father. She was injured. Honestly, Ravi, if you'd seen her… hell, I'm considering going to visit her to check on her." Heather folded her arms and watched Leo get into his car, displeasure obvious on her features.

They watched him drive away before turning back to watch the glaziers again.

"Will you?" Ravi asked.

"Will I what?"

"Go check on her?"

Heather sighed. "I don't know. I don't have a reason to. She's not my direct report, and I should probably leave her to rest. It would just be nice to know that *someone* is keeping an eye on her."

Ravi didn't say anything. Heather didn't often show this level of concern for her employees. Either Scarlett was hurt more than he knew, or Heather had developed a soft spot for the difficult-to-reach woman.

20

Bored

SCARLETT LOOKED into the bathroom mirror and frowned. Two neat stitches closed the wound near her hairline, the other cuts not requiring anything other than time in order to heal. She lifted her finger to one of the wounds and prodded the cut to test how painful they were.

She winced a little.

As she suspected, the injuries were not that bad. She'd certainly had more painful injuries in the past. Which she had attempted to explain to Heather when she was ordering her to take two days off work, but Heather had been unmovable to reason.

Scarlett let out a sigh and left the bathroom in search of something to occupy her now that she had two surprise days off to fill. She supposed she shouldn't go outside as she did look like she had been in a fight. Which wasn't far off the truth.

The book that Nico had given her sat unread on the kitchen counter. She picked it up and looked at the pink hearts and cartoon depictions of two women holding hands on the cover.

Scarlett had never been one for reading. She'd enjoyed it as a child, but as she got older she found it harder to understand character actions and motivations. It had also been a shock to discover that many people saw the book's words playing out in their mind like a personal movie being created and projected from within the brain. Scarlett had never experienced that. Books were printed words. Imagining what a character looked like or having an entire scene recreated in her mind was something that she just couldn't seem to do.

Feeling as if she was only achieving half of what the reading experience ought to be had caused her to cut back on her reading until it hardly featured in her life at all.

Her phone rang, and she saw her father's office number on the screen. She swallowed, wondering if her father was aware of what had happened and was taking the time to call her. It seemed unlikely, but the possibility still lurked in the back of her mind.

"Hello?" she answered.

"Hi Scarlett, it's Diane."

Scarlett swallowed down a small bubble of disappointment. Diane was her father's PA and the only person from her father's office who ever called, but that didn't stop Scarlett from expecting a call from him one day.

"Hello."

"I just wanted to call to remind you that it's your stepmother's birthday party at the weekend."

"Yes, I know." Scarlett didn't know why Diane insisted

on always calling to remind her about things she already knew.

"Will you be attending?"

"Yes."

"Excellent, I'll let your father know. He'll be pleased to see you."

Scarlett clamped her mouth closed. They both knew it wasn't the truth.

"I'll send you the email invite so you have all the information," Diane continued.

"Thank you," Scarlett replied, although she was unsure why Diane would bother. Scarlett was aware of all the details from the last time Diane had emailed. And the party would take place in her childhood home; it wasn't like she didn't know the address.

The line went quiet, and Scarlett suspected that Diane had little else to say. She said a goodbye and hung up the call.

Her gaze dropped to the book again. She turned it over and read the back. Apparently one of the characters was a firefighter. With nothing else on her schedule, Scarlett tentatively opened the book to the first chapter and started reading.

After thirty minutes of standing in the kitchen, she decided to take the book into the living room and sit down. The book wasn't projecting images into her mind, but she was able to follow along with the story to some degree, even if the firefighter's girlfriend's actions were a complete mystery to her. But then, almost everyone's actions were.

21

Many Glasses

YASMIN BROUGHT a mug of coffee into Heather's office and placed it on the coaster by her laptop. Heather barely looked up, too busy focusing on the spreadsheets on her screen.

"Thanks," she mumbled distractedly.

"Sorry to bother you, but Scarlett Flynn is here," Yasmin said. "She said she had an email from you to come and see her before she starts work again?"

Heather tore her eyes from the screen and looked at Yasmin. She'd sent the email the morning of the break-in; now she wondered if that had really been two days ago. In fact, time as a whole felt like more of an abstract concept to her lately.

"Is it nine already?" Heather wondered aloud.

"Ten to, she's early," Yasmin replied with a grin. She seemed to take pleasure in her boss's inability to keep up with time and dates.

"Send her in." Heather noticed the mug of steaming coffee and picked it up. "And thanks for the coffee."

"You already thanked me," Yasmin reminded her.

"Coffee demands two thanks at least," Heather joked.

Yasmin chuckled and exited Heather's office, and Heather heard a mumbled conversation before Scarlett entered the room. Heather had hoped that Scarlett would look a little bit better than she had the last time she saw her, but the cuts and bruises on her face looked just as angry.

"You wanted to see me?" Scarlett asked, standing to loose attention in front of Heather's desk.

"I did," Heather confirmed. "Take a seat."

Scarlett frowned but did as she was told.

"How are you feeling?" Heather asked, leaning back in her chair, cupping the mug of coffee in her hands.

"I'm ready to return to work."

"That's not quite what I asked," Heather pointed out. "We have facilities available to you if you need to talk about what happened."

Scarlett looked baffled. "I already gave a statement to the police."

Heather smiled. "I meant someone who could help you with any emotional feelings. I saw the CCTV footage; you were nearly killed."

Heather's stomach lurched a little at the reminder of what she had seen. It had been dark and grainy, but the image of Scarlett standing in front of the car with her hand held high as if that would stop the teenagers intent on wreaking havoc was seared into her mind. Scarlett's quick reflexes had allowed her to get out of the way before being hit, but the shower of glass was unavoidable.

"I don't feel the need to talk to anyone about what happened," Scarlett said.

"I see you got your glasses repaired," Heather said. "That was fast."

"These are not the same pair that were damaged. They were beyond repair."

"Oh, I'm sorry. They look very like your old pair."

"They are identical."

"Ah, that would explain it," Heather said. "You're lucky the optician had them in stock."

"I didn't see an optician."

Heather felt a twinge of pain in her brain. Sometimes Scarlett was extremely difficult to talk to.

"I'm not following," Heather admitted.

"I have several pairs of glasses," Scarlett elaborated. "In case something should happen to one pair."

"I see. And you have a pair that are the same?"

"They are all the same."

"You have several pairs of identical glasses?" Heather queried.

"Yes. In case something happens." Scarlett regarded Heather as if she were explaining something to a particularly slow child.

"Right," Heather said, not knowing what else to say.

"I'd like to get back to work."

Heather bit her lip. "I'd like that, too, but you look a little like you've been in a brawl. It's not a good look for a security officer on patrol."

"What do you suggest?" Scarlett asked, an edge to her tone indicating that she wasn't entirely happy with Heather's comment.

"I'll speak with Tara. I'm sure we can find you something away from the public for now. Until you've healed. As long as you're sure you are ready to be back at work?" Heather asked again, intent on giving Scarlett every opportunity to take an extra day or two if she needed it.

"I'd like to get back to work," Scarlett repeated.

"Very well." Heather knew she couldn't force Scarlett to take more time off. She clearly felt she was ready to get back to it, and Heather couldn't detect any lingering issues.

Not that Scarlett was the easiest to read at the best of times.

Heather put her coffee down and picked up the phone, dialling Tara's number.

"What did you get up to while you were off?" Heather asked Scarlett conversationally.

"I cleaned my apartment and read a book."

Tara answered the call, and Heather quickly spoke to her about Scarlett coming back to work and made arrangements for her to be office-bound for at least another week.

When she hung up, Heather tried one last-ditch effort to converse with Scarlett. "I'll be attending your mother's birthday party this weekend. I assume you'll be there?"

"Yes. But she is my stepmother," Scarlett corrected. "My mother died when I was very young; my father remarried when I was eight."

Heather wasn't sure what to say to that. It was probably one of the most personal things that Scarlett had ever said to her, but with no idea of how Scarlett felt about either of those events, Heather felt unsure how to reply.

"I see. I'm sorry to hear about your mother," she said, opting for the safest route.

"I don't remember her," Scarlett said without emotion.

Heather thought that was both heart-breaking and a blessing rolled into one. She wondered if the loss of her mother and the subsequent introduction of a new woman when she was so young explained a little of why it was so difficult to get through to Scarlett now.

She knew she was grasping for straws, trying to understand Scarlett a little better so she could know how to connect with her.

"Well, if I don't see you before, I'll see you on Saturday," Heather said to finish up the conversation that seemed to be going nowhere.

Scarlett hesitated for a beat. "We are finished?"

Heather nodded. "We are."

Scarlett jumped to her feet and hurriedly left the office. Heather watched her leave, a smile curling at the corner of her mouth.

22

Just a Loan

RAVI EXITED the large bookseller following a meeting about the refurbishment they were due to undergo. He'd barely gotten a few steps out of the store when he heard a familiar voice shout out, "Traitor!"

He smiled and turned around to see Nico at her pop-up shop, staring at him and shaking her head with mock despair.

"They're the enemy!" she called out, gesturing to the large, high-street retailer behind him.

He walked over to her. "They are a client," he corrected her.

"Can't believe you went in and spoke with the enemy," Nico grumbled playfully. She tidied some books as she shook her head. "I thought we were mates, but now I see your true colours."

Ravi laughed. "You know that you're my favourite."

"I better be," Nico told him with a wide smile.

Their playful banter came to an end as Scarlett Flynn

appeared, a book in her hand. "I'm returning the book you loaned me." She turned to look at Ravi. "The book was a loan and not a gift, which I have now returned. Therefore, I am not in breach of centre guidelines."

Ravi nodded formally. "Excellent, glad to hear it."

In truth, he knew gifts were quite common between stores and employees of The Arches Group. He generally turned a blind eye to it unless he knew it was meant more as a bribe than a gift.

Most people knew the guidelines were just that, guidance, an indication to be careful about accepting gifts in return for preferential treatment. But of course Scarlett would take the guidelines much more literally than that.

"And, welcome back, hero," he added.

Scarlett shook her head. "I'm not a hero."

Nico took the proffered book. "No, you're not. From what I hear you were stupid. You need to take care of yourself much better than that."

Scarlett blinked and stared at Nico in surprise, clearly not expecting the reprimand.

"I am a security officer, it's my job to sto—"

"Blah blah," Nico silenced her. "Not if it means risking yourself. That's just stupid. Anyway, did you like the book?"

Scarlett seemed to struggle to keep up with Nico, stuttering a little before she finally admitted, "No."

Ravi turned to face Nico, wondering what her response to that would be.

"No? What didn't you like?" Nico asked, leaning on the counter and attempting to gauge customer feedback.

"It was unrealistic."

Nico chuckled. "Well, it is a book of fiction. It's meant to take a little creative licence."

"I prefer realism."

"Okay then, I think I have something for you," Nico said, standing up and shuffling through some books in a box behind her. "It just came in, but I know the author's style."

"I don't require another book," Scarlett argued.

"Ha! Next you'll be saying you don't require food," Nico replied. She plucked a book out of the delivery box and held it out towards Scarlett.

Scarlett looked at the book and then at Ravi.

He held up his hands. "Nothing to do with me. But I warn you, I know from experience that if you don't take it now she'll hound you endlessly until you do."

Nico nodded her head seriously. "I will."

Scarlett tentatively took the book. "Very well. This is not a gift; this is a loan. It will be returned, as per centre guidelines."

Nico smothered a smile. "Absolutely. Just a loan. How about a selfie with the book? Do you feel like smiling today?"

"No," Scarlett replied honestly.

"Fair enough," Nico said. "I hope you enjoy this loan more than the previous one."

"I will let you know," Scarlett said. She inclined her head in a formal farewell to them both before leaving.

"I like her," Nico declared when Scarlett was out of earshot.

"You're one of the few," Ravi said.

"She's fun. Never know what she'll say next."

Ravi laughed. "That's definitely true."

"Now, about these meetings you're having with the enemy," Nico said, turning to Ravi with her arms folded.

23

The Party

HEATHER STEPPED out of the taxi and put her small clutch bag under her arm while she adjusted her dress. She hoped it wasn't too creased from the car journey; it had been a while since she'd worn a cocktail dress. In the hour since she'd put it on, she'd nearly spilt something on it and almost split a seam. She hoped she remembered how to woman before she embarrassed herself.

As she expected, Leo Flynn lived in what could only be described as a mansion. It was located just outside of London, near enough to grant him fast access to the city but quiet enough to be considered rural.

She walked through the open iron gates and past the well-tended front garden. The large, double front doors were open, and she could see into the hallway where guests mingled with champagne flutes.

Heather sucked in a quick, fortifying breath before stepping into the house.

"There she is!" a loud voice bellowed.

She plastered on her best smile and turned to greet Leo.

"This is the woman who is going to teach me how to make shopping centres profitable," he said loudly to the group he had been speaking with.

Heather chuckled. "Well, I hope so, at least!"

The group politely smiled and laughed. Heather was quickly introduced to them all, knowing immediately that she wouldn't remember a single one of them. But she did what was required of her and smiled and shook hands with everyone she was introduced to.

Interestingly, most of the guests seemed to be business acquaintances of Leo's rather than friends and family members. Heather knew that a business colleague could also be a friend, but it seemed very obvious to her that the party served a dual purpose: a birthday party and a networking opportunity.

After an hour Heather had mingled with most people and found her way to the kitchen to introduce herself to Audrey Flynn, Leo's wife.

Audrey seemed genuinely pleased to see her and took Heather's outstretched hand in both of hers.

"It's so wonderful to finally meet you. Leo has spoken about you."

"Some good, I hope?" Heather asked, chuckling.

"All good. Which is rare for Leo." Audrey gestured to Heather's empty glass. "Can I get you some more champagne?"

Heather placed the glass on the kitchen counter with a group of other empties. "No, thank you. I'm not much of a drinker."

"There's plenty of orange juice going around," Audrey said. "And we have a stash of cranberry juice for Scarlett, but she won't mind sharing, I'm sure."

"I've not seen Scarlett," Heather said. She didn't want to admit it, but she had been looking for the young woman and had been increasingly disappointed to not see her in the crowds.

"She doesn't like parties; she's here somewhere but probably skulking in a corner somewhere. Until Leo forces her to say hello to a few people, at least." Audrey picked up a canapé and took a small bite. "I was surprised to see her when she arrived; I didn't know she had been injured at work."

Heather couldn't help but raise her eyebrow in surprise.

"Leo and Scarlett don't really speak," Audrey explained before Heather had a chance to say anything.

"So I'm realising," Heather said diplomatically.

"I've tried to get them to be closer, but, well, it's not always easy with family, is it?"

"No, not always," Heather agreed.

But she didn't really agree. To her, family was the easiest thing. The most important thing, too. It ached in her that Scarlett didn't have that support network that Heather relied on so much.

"She's a good girl, though," Audrey said.

Heather detected a warmth from Audrey and decided that she wasn't the evil stepmother that fairy tales would have people assume.

"She is," Heather agreed. "She's a fine addition to our team."

Audrey almost sagged with relied. "Oh, I am so glad to hear that. I don't ask Leo because, well, he doesn't know and wouldn't want to discuss it even if he did. And Scarlett isn't the easiest to talk to either. Which I'm sure you've noticed."

Heather couldn't have agreed more. She was partly pleased that someone else also had trouble talking to Scarlett but was also saddened by the fact. Especially considering it was one of Scarlett's parents.

"Sorry to interrupt," Leo said as he appeared in the kitchen. "Audrey, Kathy wants to know which florist you chose in the end for the summer garden party?"

Audrey placed her hand on Heather's arm apologetically. "I'm sorry, I have to stop a literal war of roses happening. I hope we can speak more later."

Heather smiled. "Absolutely."

Following directions from another guest, Heather walked up the large staircase of the Flynn house to locate a bathroom. The one downstairs seemed constantly occupied due to the sheer number of people at the party.

Hanging around the downstairs bathroom only meant getting pulled into more conversations, and one thing was becoming abundantly clear: it wasn't *just* a birthday party.

Heather had engaged in fewer work-related conversations during business conferences. Every little group was discussing something to do with economic projections, financial lending, buyouts, or investments.

Thankfully, Heather was well versed in such conversations and could hold her own, but that didn't mean it wasn't boring to say the least.

After locating and using a bathroom, she noticed a familiar figure in one of the rooms off the hallway.

She paused in the doorway and took a moment to look at Scarlett, who was standing in the middle of the room with her back to the door. Heather had never seen Scarlett with her hair down and found herself staring at the perfect, soft curls.

Sensing she was being observed, Scarlett turned.

Heather swallowed at the sight of the figure-hugging red dress.

Scarlett simply raised an eyebrow, questioning Heather's presence.

"Having a good time?" Heather asked.

"No," Scarlett replied, a hint of sarcasm in her otherwise honest tone.

Heather laughed and stepped into the room. "Hiding?"

Scarlett nodded. She gestured to the room and the floor-to-ceiling bookshelves. "This was once my bedroom."

Heather thought it odd that a house with so many rooms would convert a child's bedroom into a library. Her own childhood bedroom had been sacrificed to a spare bedroom for guests, but that was necessary due to a lack of space.

"My old bedroom is a guest room," Heather said, "which I use when I go down there. It's quite surreal."

"You would prefer it to be the way it was?" Scarlett asked.

Heather smiled at the memory of her old bedroom: the

posters of bands, the mess of clothes, the guitar she had never learned to play leaning against the wall.

"No, it's probably better the way it is. Do you miss your bedroom?"

Scarlett looked around the room thoughtfully. "It's unsettling to see it so different. Especially as my brother's room remains a bedroom."

Heather raised her eyebrow in surprise. "I didn't know you had a brother?"

"He died."

Heather's breath caught in her chest.

"Suicide," Scarlett added.

"I'm so sorry to hear that," Heather said, licking her suddenly dry lips. She noticed that Scarlett's expression had hardly changed despite dropping what could only be described as bombshell-level news.

"It was difficult," Scarlett acknowledged.

Heather felt her heart break on Scarlett's behalf, wondering if Scarlett's cold exterior was simply a coping mechanism. Death of a mother and a brother, who could cope with such horrendous circumstances?

Heather couldn't imagine what sort of toll such loss would have on a person, or on a family. Perhaps she was seeing the results of it.

"Ah, there you are," Leo said, addressing Scarlett as he stepped into the room. "You need to mingle with the guests whether you like it or not."

Heather couldn't believe the terrible timing Leo had. She was finally having an actual conversation with Scarlett. The young woman had seemed on the verge of opening up, and here was Leo, essentially ruining the moment.

She cast a glance to Scarlett, noticing an almost military stiffness in her spine at the appearance of her father.

"I will mingle now," Scarlett agreed readily, leaving the room in a clipped stride.

Leo sighed and pinched the bridge of his nose.

"She's fitting in well," Heather said, suddenly needing to defend Scarlett and prove to Leo that she wasn't the awkward and difficult woman he seemed to assume she was.

Leo looked at her questioningly.

"Scarlett," Heather explained. "She's fitting in very well at Silver Arches. I've heard excellent feedback from her line manager."

That much was true at least. Tara did have a lot of good to say about Scarlett; unfortunately, it was usually followed by a complaint of her social ineptitude. But Heather wouldn't mention that now. It had suddenly become important for her to convince Leo that his daughter was doing well.

Leo looked a little flustered but undeniably pleased. "Good, that's nice to hear."

"I know you had your concerns about her fitting in," Heather said, attempting to fish for more information.

"I do. But I see she's in good hands."

"She is," Heather promised.

A female voice called out for Leo's attention, and he gestured that he had to go. Once he left the room, Heather let out a heavy sigh. She'd told a white lie, but one that meant she had to make sure that Scarlett did fit in.

Unfortunately, she wasn't entirely sure how she was going to manage that.

24

Don't Want to Be Friends

SCARLETT MOVED from group to group in the downstairs of the house, allocating three to five minutes to each group before moving on. She'd been forced to socialise with these people ever since she was old enough to stay up for one of her father's frequent parties.

She knew the drill well. Enter a group, say hello to the members of the group, and ask a vague question about a family member of one person. Listen to the answer, and then provide a small insight into her own work life. Then it was simply a matter of waiting for someone to tell a joke or amusing story, and then laugh and make a discreet exit by pretending she had seen someone else she had to say hello to.

Occasionally she was cornered by the professional photographer that her father had hired to document the event. The man had taken a shine to her, pulling her into groups to have her photo taken, and ordering her to smile.

The concept of having to smile for photographs was one she found truly baffling.

As a child she was frequently asked to smile for photos despite the fact she was not at all happy. The result was photo albums filled with lies. Family holidays, birthday parties, and more, all filled with fake, hollow smiles. Not a real depiction of events at all.

When she became a teenager, Scarlett decided to stop smiling for photos unless she was honestly happy. She wasn't trying to be awkward despite what her father thought. She just didn't like the dishonesty of it all.

Scarlett had calculated that she'd be around all the current groups in around sixty-five minutes. Then she could consider her duty done, and she would be able to disappear back home.

Her plan came to an abrupt end when she noticed someone unexpected in the next group she intended to join.

Rather than making her way to that group, she made a beeline for the utility room off the kitchen. It was one of the few places that guests weren't congregating, and it allowed her a few moments of peace to consider what she had just seen and what, if anything, to do about it.

Steph, her ex, was at the party.

Neither Audrey nor her father had told her that Steph would be there. Scarlett certainly hadn't invited her, and so she was at a loss to explain her presence.

Familiar feelings of loss and confusion hit her.

The breakup was old news to most, but Scarlett still

dwelled on the end of the relationship. It had been a failure, apparently one of her own making. Steph had said she had stayed as long as she could, indicating she had been unhappy for a long time.

Scarlett had been blindsided by the whole thing.

The utility room door opened, and Steph peeked through the gap at her. "Can I come in?"

Scarlett realised she had been seen making her escape and wished she had gone into the garden instead. At least that way she would have been able to lose Steph in the crowd rather than be stuck in a room with no exit.

Steph stepped into the room and closed the door behind her without Scarlett inviting her in.

"Hey," Steph greeted.

Scarlett didn't reply. Didn't know *what* to reply.

"I'm assuming your dad didn't tell you I'd be here?" Steph continued.

"My father doesn't tell me much," Scarlett pointed out sarcastically. Steph knew that, of course.

"Yeah, I should have expected that. I'm working for him now. Well, for Intrex. He sought me out and asked if I wanted a role when my contract was up. I was going to tell you, but, well, we don't really speak."

"We broke up."

"We could still be friends," Steph suggested.

Scarlett wasn't sure they could.

The end of the relationship had been difficult, and she wasn't certain she could push those feelings to one side and have a friendship with someone who had so thoroughly broken her heart.

"I'm sorry about the way things ended," Steph said, as if reading her mind.

"You're not," Scarlett replied, feeling hurt emotions swirling around her.

"I... we weren't right for each other. It wasn't working," Steph admitted. "But I didn't want to hurt you."

"You did hurt me."

"I know, and I'm sorry. I should have handled things differently. I shouldn't have said some of the things I said," Steph said, "but maybe we can put those things behind us and be friends?"

Scarlett swallowed.

She didn't *want* to be friends. She wasn't even very good at being someone's friend. Not to mention the fact that her excellent memory played over Steph's hurtful last words to her every time she saw or thought of Steph.

But this seemed to be a time when Scarlett was expected to push her feelings to one side in order to bend to societal norms.

She'd lost count of the number of times in her life that she had been told she had to do something even though she desperately didn't want to. Being normal, her father referred to it.

Scarlett didn't know what that meant, but she did know that it often meant she had to do something that she didn't want to do in order to please others. Being normal seemed to always involve Scarlett making a sacrifice. She didn't understand it, and she didn't like it.

The utility room door opened once more, and Audrey entered the room.

"I thought I saw you come in here, Steph," Audrey said. "Leo is looking for you."

"Oh, okay," Steph said. She looked at Scarlett and smiled softly. "Maybe catch up with you later?"

Scarlett didn't say anything. She didn't want to catch up with Steph later. Or ever again. Although she suspected the new proximity of her ex-girlfriend to her father might make that impossible.

Steph left, and Audrey closed the door behind her.

"Are you okay?" Audrey asked.

Scarlett wished people would understand that she rarely knew the answer to that question. She gave a small shrug.

Audrey pulled her into a hug, and Scarlett felt a sense of relief. She hadn't known she wanted a hug, but the moment Audrey enveloped her in one, it felt right.

"I didn't know Leo had invited her. I'm sorry," Audrey whispered. "I know it must be hard to see her."

"It is," Scarlett agreed.

Audrey stepped back and took Scarlett's face in her hands. "I hope you know that if you ever need me, my door is always open to you."

"I know," Scarlett said.

And while she was aware of that fact, the truth was that she wouldn't know what to say.

She appreciated Audrey's continuous offers of help but felt powerless to accept them.

25

Interrupting Breakfast

HEATHER WAS MILDLY surprised to find Leo sitting in her office on Monday morning. No meeting was in the diary, and the last she'd heard from him was that she'd speak to him by telephone towards the end of the week.

"Good morning," she greeted him as she put her bag under her desk and placed her coffee and breakfast on the desk.

"We need to think of expansion plans," Leo said without hesitation. He'd clearly been waiting a while and was eager to get into the conversation.

"What kind of expansion?" Heather asked.

She turned on her computer and started to set up for the day in much the same way she would if he wasn't there. If Leo wasn't going to call ahead, then he was going to have to take her as she was. She suspected Leo was trying to play some ridiculous game of office politics with her. If he thought she'd defer to him in some way in her own office, he had another thing coming.

She opened the takeaway bag and took out her breakfast croissant.

"Experiences," he said. "That's what people want. Retail shopping goes up and down, and people can buy a lot online these days. Their appetite for buying online will only increase. But experiences, that's where we need to focus."

"Agreed," Heather said, taking the first bite of her unhealthy but delicious breakfast. "People need to eat, and cafe culture is becoming more and more popular. Restaurants struggle from time to time, but only because there is an abundance of them. But the cinema, bowling, those kinds of things seem to be thriving."

"We need to go further," Leo said. "We need to consider what kind of experiences people want and, more importantly, what they can't get elsewhere. I remember when laser tag was big. Do we try to bring it back? Or is there new tech out there? We need a team of people from all backgrounds to bounce ideas around."

"Sounds like an excellent idea," Heather said, taking another bite of croissant.

She had been worried that Leo would be another out-of-touch investor who would have an idea and run with it no matter what. Instead, he seemed eager to crowdsource ideas from a variety of people and combine those findings with his own research to come up with plans. Utilising his business experience alongside advice he received in a sensible manner.

"Justin Freeman is our head of entertainment, and Lucy Williams is our experiences manager," Heather said. "Then I think we should canvass some of the younger people in the teams. Maybe find some people from each department to get a wide selection of people. Ravi has his finger on the pulse; Thomas Kingsley is known for being the most frugal man in the company—if he thinks something is worth spending his money, then we're in the right area. Scarlett would be a good addition too—"

"No, not Scarlett," Leo said quickly.

"Maybe she'll surprise you?" Heather suggested.

Leo laughed. "She's surprised me every single day since she was born."

"Well, she certainly thinks out of the box, and that's what a project like this needs," Heather pushed.

"Scarlett and I don't work together, and that's that," Leo said firmly.

Heather thought for a moment about how she wanted to handle the order. Within a few short seconds, her mind was made up and she'd put her croissant down. "I don't allow personal feuds to prevent working relationships in my centre," she said with dead seriousness. "I expect everyone to be able to work together. Wouldn't you agree that is an important factor in a team?"

Leo maintained strict eye contact. Heather matched him, not blinking. A few tense seconds passed before a grin formed on his face.

"You're fearless, you know that?" he said.

Heather took another bite of food and shrugged. "Honest, is all."

"I love Scarlett. I do, with all my heart," Leo admitted. "But she drives me crazy and I don't like the person she makes me become when we spend too much time together."

Heather frowned. "What do you mean?"

"She infuriates me," Leo explained. "I get angry. You may have heard rumours about me shouting and throwing things, but they are rarely true. But Scarlett, she pushes a button in me. I find her… I find her illogical. And cold. So… devoid of feeling. I can't get through to her, and she's my daughter."

Heather was surprised but pleased by the admission. Finally, she felt like she was getting somewhere in figuring out the rift between father and daughter. She didn't know why it was important to her, but it was. She felt like it would be an incredible victory to bring the two together, if such a thing was at all possible.

"I'll admit that it is a little hard to understand her behaviour sometimes," Heather allowed, "but I don't find her to be devoid of feeling. Perhaps a little reluctant to share them, but she definitely feels things. I'm sure of that."

Leo let out a sigh. "Audrey suspects she's autistic."

Heather's eyes widened. "Oh." She didn't know what else to say. It made a lot of sense. She didn't know why she hadn't thought of it before. It was like a critical puzzle piece falling into place.

"She's hardly old, but when she went through school it wasn't really something they tested for. She got through school okay, no friends and one or two detentions for talking back to her teachers, but nothing dramatic," Leo explained. "People weren't talking about autism when Scarlett was growing up. It's only in recent years that it's really in the public eye."

"Have you discussed it with Scarlett?" Heather asked.

Leo shook his head. "As I said, we don't speak."

"Maybe clearing the air…"

Leo shifted uncomfortably in his seat. "No. Look, we're getting off topic. I'm not here to talk about Scarlett. I want a list of names for a think tank, at least fifteen people. And definitely not Scarlett."

Heather knew when to push a subject further and when to remain quiet, and this was definitely the latter.

"I'll get a list to you by this afternoon," she promised.

Leo stood up and plucked his phone out of his inner jacket pocket, looking like his attention was fully absorbed in his work. Heather suspected it was a ruse to aid his escape.

"Great, great," he said distractedly. "I need to get back to my office."

He was gone without another glance at her.

Heather pushed her croissant away, suddenly losing her appetite.

She knew next to nothing about autism other than what she'd heard in popular media. On top of that, she only had Audrey's suspicion to go on.

She didn't even know why it was relevant to her. Scarlett was doing well in security, not making any friends but certainly not making as many enemies as she had done before. Could that be considered a victory? Making fewer enemies? Mathematically, it brought her closer to fitting in, Heather considered.

However, there was a strong urge in Heather to help Scarlett more. She didn't like the idea of the woman being lonely or disliked. If she could get to the bottom of the mystery of Scarlett Flynn and maybe offer some help, then she would.

26

A Chat over Coffee

RAVI LIFTED his phone and took a picture of the coffee and brownie in front of him. He'd recently started using Instagram at Nico's insistence, but the only pictures he ever posted were of his mid-morning snack at one of the coffee shops in the centre.

He didn't have many followers but told himself that by tagging the business in question, he was in some way helping them with their social media marketing.

It was a long shot. He didn't really understand how little actions equated to big changes.

"What do you know about autism?"

He looked up as Heather sat down at the table with him, a takeaway coffee in her hand.

"Hi, yes, you can join me," he joked.

She ignored his quip and sipped at her coffee, looking at him over the top of the cup.

"Not a lot," he said, picking up the brownie and taking a bite. "Why?"

"I just heard from Leo that Scarlett's mother—stepmother—thinks that Scarlett may be autistic. I don't know much about it. I googled it, but there's a lot of contradicting information."

Ravi took another bite of brownie and regarded his boss and friend. Heather's growing obsession with Scarlett was intriguing.

"Why don't you ask Scarlett?" Ravi suggested.

Heather made a face. "That might not go down too well. I don't think Leo or Audrey have broached the notion with Scarlett, so it's hardly my place to do so."

"You think Scarlett might not know?" Ravi asked.

Heather shrugged. "I'm not sure. I don't want to offend her by asking. I'm not close enough to her."

Ravi quickly finished off the brownie and wiped his fingers on a napkin. "Maybe speak to Nico. She seems to have developed a sort of friendship with Scarlett."

Heather looked surprised. "Nico? Friends with Scarlett?"

Ravi chuckled. "Well, friends might be pushing it a little. But they talk, which is more than Scarlett seems to do with other people."

Heather looked thoughtful. "That makes sense, Nico does chat with everyone."

"May I ask why it's important to you?" Ravi asked.

Heather hesitated a moment, and Ravi wondered if Heather even knew herself. He knew Heather had a big heart. He also knew that Heather was lonely and couldn't resist a mystery.

"I think Scarlett is struggling," Heather explained. "And I'd like to help her if I can."

Ravi wanted to push the point and ask exactly what

had given her the idea that Scarlett was struggling. He couldn't imagine that the cool, collected security officer had gone to Heather seeking assistance.

No, this seemed to be Heather wanting to pull Scarlett into the family environment she had built up amongst Silver Arches staff.

"Are you sure she's struggling?" Ravi asked. "I've tried to get her to socialise with people and she's declined. Claimed she's happier to not socialise. I don't understand it, but I respect it."

Heather looked thoughtfully at the lid of her coffee. "I don't honestly know if she's struggling or not, but I feel that she might be. I'll feel better once I know either way. I just have a sixth sense that there's more I can do to help her."

"And you think knowing more about autism, if she does indeed have it, will help that?" Ravi fished.

Heather shrugged. "She... socialises differently to so many others. Interacts differently. It's causing a wedge between her and nearly everyone else. If I knew the reason why, then maybe I could figure out a way to help her."

"Maybe she doesn't want any help." Ravi continued to play devil's advocate.

Heather looked like she wanted to burst out laughing at that. "You think she's happy with almost everyone disliking her?"

"I don't know," Ravi admitted, "but I'm not forcing my own perception of things on her. Especially not if she is autistic. I don't know much about autism, but I do know that some people view things differently. Some people see an evening at home as lonely; some see it as bliss."

Heather placed her cup on the table and tapped the plastic top, still deep in thought. "Maybe you're right," she allowed. "Maybe I'm projecting my own feelings onto her. That's not fair; I'll have to keep an eye on that."

Ravi sipped his coffee. He'd given Heather something to think about, but he knew that wouldn't slow her down. Whenever Heather made a decision to do something, she did it. How that would play out with Scarlett, he had no idea.

27

Friday

HEATHER DOODLED on her notepad as Simon from marketing finished talking about the upcoming online campaign his team was running.

It wasn't that she wasn't interested in what he was saying, more that she didn't understand impressions and cost-per-clicks. Simon was a numbers man, enjoying going into every small detail of every campaign he ran. Heather was a results person, finding happiness in seeing more footfall.

It didn't help that it was Friday morning and she was eagerly anticipating leaving work early that day to spend the weekend with her parents.

"Sounds great. Thanks so much for that update, Simon," Ravi interrupted as Simon attempted to dive into the analytics of his social media strategy.

Everyone around the table knew that if Simon had his way, he'd talk for the entire hour allocated for the weekly head-of-department meeting.

"Is there anything else pressing?" Heather asked before

Simon had a chance to suggest he wasn't finished speaking.

Heads shook and Heather flipped her notebook shut to indicate the end of the meeting.

"Just a quick reminder that I'm out of the office this afternoon, so if you need anything please direct it to Ravi," Heather added as everyone filed out of the room.

Ravi remained seated, and Heather looked curiously at him.

"I have news," he confessed.

"Good news or bad news?" Heather asked.

He looked to the door to check everyone had left before turning back to Heather and lowering his voice. "Aurelie is coming back here."

Heather's breath caught. "Here here?"

"Yes. I didn't know how you'd feel about it, but I wanted you to hear it from me first," Ravi added.

"Thank you," Heather breathed.

"Have you spoken to her... since the break-up?" Ravi asked.

Heather shook her head. After their break-up, Aurelie had applied for an immediate transfer to the head office and had remained there ever since. They worked in the same company but never heard from each other, which suited Heather just fine. She suspected it suited Aurelie too.

"Why now?" Heather asked.

"I'm not sure. She's been at head office for three years, maybe she wants a change? Or maybe it's a promotion? I didn't find out many details, just that she's coming back here. Are you okay with that?"

"I'll have to be," Heather said. "When?"

"Monday," Ravi said apologetically.

Heather slumped in her chair. "That soon?"

"It's been in the works for a while. I only heard about it last night at the pub. Still, at least you have this afternoon and the weekend off." Ravi grabbed his belongings. "I have to go; I have a meeting with Christine about cleaning products."

"Have fun," Heather joked.

"Come say goodbye before you swan off down to Hastings," he told her before leaving the meeting room.

Heather let out a deep sigh and leaned her head back into the leather headrest of the conference room chair.

As if Intrex and Leo weren't enough to deal with at work. Now her ex was coming back to Silver Arches.

———

"Ah, there you are!"

Heather stopped walking and turned to see Nico waving her down. She smiled and walked over to the small pop-up shop of Gay Days Books.

"How are you, Nico?" Heather asked.

"I'm great. Business is good," Nico said. "I have a book to lend you."

"Lend me?" Heather asked. "Aren't you meant to be *selling* books?"

"This is how I get you hooked," Nico explained. "It's like a free sample of chocolate. Trust me, this works. I've gotten some of my best customers this way."

Heather laughed. "How about I buy one, but you recommend which one I buy?"

Heather liked Nico and wanted to support her. She didn't get to her shop as often as she would like, but she knew LGBTQ spaces were important.

In her youth she had attended LGBTQ bars and small theatre productions, but as she got older she had stopped going. Then the venues started to close, and Heather felt guilty for not supporting them.

When new bars popped up, she considered going but quickly quashed the idea. It just wasn't her scene anymore. But if someone opened a lesbian coffee shop, she'd be there in a flash. She'd probably be their number-one customer.

"I'm happy to lend you one," Nico replied.

"And I'm happy to buy one," Heather countered. "So, what do you recommend? What's hot at the moment?"

Nico scrunched up her face and started looking at the selection of books on the counter and on the wall racks.

"Hmm," Nico said, deep in thought.

"Aren't you going to ask me what types of books I like?" Heather asked.

"Nah." Nico waved that away quickly. "I have a feel for these things. It's an ability; all good bookshop owners have it."

Heather laughed and waited for Nico to magically divine which book would suit her. A moment later Nico nodded to herself and picked up a paperback and handed it to Heather.

Heather turned it over and read the back, quickly deciphering it was a contemporary lesbian romance. Not something she would often pick up, but she assumed it would be a nice and easy read.

"Scarlett's reading it at the moment," Nico said. "I'm not sure what her verdict is yet."

Heather looked up at Nico. "Scarlett? Flynn?"

Nico nodded.

"She's reading a… romance?"

"With a little arm-twisting," Nico admitted. "She didn't like the first one I suggested, but I have a very good feeling about this one."

Heather didn't know if she was more surprised to hear that Scarlett was reading a romance or that it was a lesbian romance. She wondered if she was queer or just open-minded.

It wasn't really her place to ask Nico, but the question still nagged her.

"Sounds good. I'll take it," Heather said.

Nico bagged up the book and rang up the sale on her iPad while Heather paid by card. Nico added a rainbow badge and a bookmark to the bag and handed it over to Heather.

Nico looked at her watch. "Actually, it's Scarlett's lunchtime, so she'll probably be in the food court reading it right now. If you want a reading buddy."

Heather looked at her watch and realised that it was later than she had thought. She was technically off work.

"I don't think Scarlett would want a reading buddy," Heather admitted.

"Maybe. Maybe not. Everyone needs someone to talk to now and then, even if they seem like they don't want to."

"I hear that some people like their privacy and solitude," Heather replied, a grin on her face.

"Sounds awful," Nico joked. "But, seriously, Scarlett is good to chat to if you take the lead."

Heather didn't know if that was true or not, but it was all the encouragement she needed to go and say hello to Scarlett anyway.

"Thank you for the book," Heather said and headed towards the food court.

In the food court she quickly located Scarlett at her usual table. She picked up a pre-packaged sandwich and a drink and made her way over to see Scarlett.

"May I join you?"

Scarlett looked up from her lunch and slowly nodded. As Heather sat down, she noticed it was exactly the same lunch, laid out in exactly the same way, as the last time she'd seen her in the food court.

A small voice reminded her that some of her research had indicated a desire in autistic people to follow similar patterns.

She shook the thought from her mind. She didn't know if Scarlett was autistic, and it wasn't her place to analyse her.

"Are you well?" Heather asked casually.

"Yes."

Heather smiled to herself at the lack of a detailed answer or a question as to her own health. She pointed to the book Scarlett had placed on the table.

"Nico just sold me that very book."

"We have a… lending arrangement," Scarlett explained.

"Which is in line with centre guidelines on gifts and bribes."

"I'm sure it is," Heather agreed. "What do you think of the book so far?"

Scarlett's cheeks reddened a little, and Heather was surprised and intrigued. She wondered if the content was a little more risqué than the cover indicated.

"It wasn't my... thing," Scarlett said.

Heather wanted to ask more, but there was something about Scarlett's tone and behaviour that told her now wasn't the time to push. Heather knew all too well that conversations could easily come to a stop with Scarlett if one wasn't careful.

But she couldn't help but wonder why Scarlett hadn't enjoyed the book. Was it too graphic? Was Scarlett straight?

"You're off work this weekend, aren't you?" Heather asked, briefly wondering when she had become aware of Scarlett's schedule.

"I am."

"Any exciting plans?" Heather asked.

"No."

Heather laughed. "Okay. Do you have any *un*exciting plans?"

Scarlett seemed confused by Heather's laugh and frowned. "No, I have no exciting or unexciting plans."

"You must have some plans," Heather pushed.

Scarlett looked like she wanted to sigh at Heather's continued attempts at conversation, but she didn't, which Heather thought was progress.

"I may clean my kitchen," Scarlett allowed.

"All weekend?" Heather drawled.

"Maybe. It will depend on how dirty it is."

"Do you leave it to get dirty?" Heather asked.

"No. I cleaned it last week."

"So it's likely to not be very dirty at all?" Heather pressed.

"I will see this weekend," Scarlett replied.

Heather chuckled. "Sounds like a very uninteresting weekend to me. Are you looking forward to it?"

Scarlett seemed to consider the question for a moment before she softly shook her head. "No, not really."

"Why don't you do something fun? You have your employee discount for here. You can watch a movie at the cinema? Or do some shopping?"

"I don't find those activities much fun."

Before Heather had a chance to think what she was asking she spoke. "Do you like dogs?"

"Yes, very much." Scarlett's eyes twinkled with interest. It was the first real excitement Heather had ever seen the woman demonstrate.

Heather paused for a second. The invitation was on the tip of her tongue. An internal battle warred for a few moments before her heart won out.

"I'm going to Hastings this weekend to see my parents. They run a dog rescue charity. Why don't you come down? You could spend the day with us on Saturday. There are frequent trains from London to Hastings, only an hour or two's journey. You can help me walk some dogs along the cliffs, get some fresh air. What do you think? That's more fun than cleaning your already clean kitchen, isn't it?"

For a moment Scarlett looked at Heather as if she had lost her mind, and Heather wondered if she had. Her parents wouldn't mind her inviting a member of staff to join them for the day; she'd invited people before, but they were staff members who had become friends, people like Ravi. Not people she hardly knew like Scarlett.

It wasn't an invitation she extended to many people. She could count on one hand the number of people who even knew her parents ran the charity, and now she was inviting the most aloof person she'd ever met.

She wondered if she should retract the invitation before the situation became more uncomfortable.

"Yes," Scarlett said unexpectedly. "I would like that."

Heather did her best to cover up her shock. She hadn't expected Scarlett to agree; in fact, she'd expected Scarlett to cite some buried line from the centre rules handbook that said the centre director absolutely mustn't ever invite someone she hardly knew to her parents for the weekend.

But Scarlett had said yes. And she'd said she'd *like* it. Heather didn't have to search her memory to know that Scarlett had never said she would like something before.

Any hesitation drifted away as she got her phone out of her pocket.

"What's your number? I'll text you to arrange the details."

Scarlett quickly reeled off the digits and Heather saved them.

"I'll drop you a note later on tonight," Heather said.

Her eyes caught the clock in the corner of the phone, and she realised she'd better hurry if she was going to miss the Friday afternoon traffic.

"I have to go; I'm running late as usual." Heather picked up her lunch and stood up. "I'll see you tomorrow."

Scarlett said goodbye and then returned to something she was reading on her phone.

As Heather walked through the food court, she wondered what exactly she'd tell her parents.

It was going to be an interesting weekend.

28

Welcome to Ore

SCARLETT ATTEMPTED to ignore the two women in the train carriage who were having a very loud conversation about their teenage boys' inability to clean.

It was difficult to tune them out, even though she had her headphones in and soft jazz music played in her ears. Scarlett wasn't necessarily a fan of jazz music but found that the many different beats of the songs aided in covering up the incessant, repetitive rattle of the train.

Unfortunately, it did little to cover the sound of middle-aged women who would clearly have been happier if they had never got married and had children.

She shifted in her seat and focused her attention on the countryside whizzing by outside the window. It hadn't taken long for the busy streets of London to melt away and the countryside of Sussex to take its place.

A brief text conversation the evening before had led to her boarding the nine o'clock train and planning to meet Heather at a train station called Ore an hour and a half later.

Scarlett was baffled as to why Heather had invited her and even more confused about why she had agreed. She had initially wondered if the invitation was an order from her boss, but upon reflection she doubted that was the case.

It had occurred to her that, while not an order, the invitation could still be work-related.

It seemed very unlikely, though not impossible, that Heather would involve her parents in any business discussions with members of staff. There was also the fact that if Heather had wanted to have a conversation away from the office, there were easier locations.

Scarlett couldn't fathom why Heather would want to have a conversation with her. Tara, as her line manager, would surely be the individual who would speak with her if anything needed to be said.

She had very nearly cancelled, but curiosity had gotten the better of her. And the awareness that, if the invitation was to talk about work, the work talk would no doubt happen at some point anyway.

She turned up the music, from eight to twelve. It was a little too loud, but she couldn't stand the idea of the volume being set to eleven. She closed her eyes and leaned her head against the window, waiting for Ore.

Scarlett got off the train and looked around the station. It was small, just two long concrete platforms and a tiny ticket office.

To one side of the train tracks lay fields; the other held

a newly built housing development. Unlike London stations, there were no ticket barriers, staff, or many other passengers.

She saw Heather strolling towards her; she wore light blue jeans and a thin, checked shirt with the sleeves rolled up. Her hands were in the back pockets of her jeans, and she looked casual and relaxed, very different to the centre director that Scarlett was used to seeing.

"You look younger and more relaxed in casual clothing," Scarlett told her.

Heather burst out laughing. "Thank you, I think."

"It was a compliment," Scarlett assured her, unsure why the comment had caused Heather to laugh or doubt her sincerity.

"You look lovely too," Heather said. "Shall we get to the car?"

Scarlett looked down at her black jeans and plain white T-shirt and wondered what was lovely about her outfit. It was what she wore any weekend she wasn't working, but she'd never had a compliment on it before.

Rather than question it, she followed Heather down a series of wheelchair-accessible ramps. They arrived at an old Jeep that was caked in mud that looked like it had been building up for years.

"My dad doesn't believe in cleaning cars," Heather explained. "He says they'll only get dirty again."

"He's right."

"Oh, he's going to like you." Heather laughed and got into the car.

Scarlett also got into the car and mentally reminded

herself of her conversation starters she had prepared for Heather's parents.

Social interaction was often a difficult process for her, and so, at age thirteen, Scarlett had started preparing topics and jokes before she met new people.

She wondered if she should attempt the jokes on Heather first, to check that they were appropriate. The website had declared they were clean and inoffensive, but Scarlett had been burnt in the past.

She decided to take the risk rather than have Heather hear the jokes twice.

"It's only five minutes away," Heather said, starting the engine and driving off.

"Why did you invite me?" Scarlett asked. The question had been on the tip of her tongue since Heather had done so. This had been the first opportunity to actually ask and put any fears to rest.

"It's what friends do," Heather replied.

"We're friends?" Scarlett asked, surprised but delighted at the news.

"I think we are, or at least we will be," Heather said.

Scarlett smiled at that.

She turned to watch the housing development change into rolling fields and farmland. She didn't know when or how she had become friends with Heather, but she was glad of the fact. It allowed her to relax a little and try to enjoy whatever the day was to bring.

It was nine, nearly ten, minutes later when they arrived at farm. Scarlett made a mental note to ignore Heather's future time estimates.

There was a large building which Scarlett assumed

was the main house, and then there was a barn which seemed to house equipment rather than animals. In the distance she could see a few other buildings and assumed they were the kennels. The sound of distant barking certainly indicated that was the case.

An older man and woman came out of the house, and Scarlett felt herself freeze with nervous anticipation. She'd sucked in a deep breath as the Jeep came to a stop.

The man opened her car door and smiled warmly at her.

"Hello, you must be Scarlett. I'm Mike. Welcome!"

"Thank you," Scarlett said, getting out of the car.

Mike gestured to the woman beside him. "This is my wife, Sue."

"We're so pleased you could come," Sue said. "Can I get you a drink? I've just put the kettle on."

Scarlett nodded. "Yes. Thank you."

She followed Sue towards the house, and Mike came up beside her.

"So, do you like dogs, Scarlett?"

"I do. I had one when I was younger," Scarlett said. The older rescue dog had only been with them for a few short years before she became ill and had to be put to sleep, but Scarlett remembered her fondly.

"Excellent. We have eighteen dogs onsite at the moment." Mike held the farmhouse door open and gestured for her to go inside. "Plenty of walking and cuddling to be done."

"She's a guest, Mike, not a worker," Sue told him.

"It's hardly work," Mike replied.

"I'm happy to do it," Scarlett said.

"Don't let my father bully you. Before you know it, you'll be re-roofing the old kennel block," Heather whispered a tad too loudly for Mike to not be able to hear.

"That would be a mistake. I don't know how to install a new roof," Scarlett told her.

Everyone chuckled, and Mike tapped Scarlett on the shoulder. "I like you."

Scarlett didn't know what she had done to be deserving of Mike's praise, but she felt a small flame of happiness flickering in her stomach.

She sat at the large dining table while Sue made drinks and Mike and Heather playfully bantered with one another.

Adjusting her glasses, she looked around the kitchen. It was clean, comfortable, and looked like the hub of an active, happy family. She didn't know how she knew that, but everything radiated a warmth that she'd never seen or felt before.

She looked at the floor; it was worn flagstone, which indicated a lot of family traffic. The worktops were equally well used, loved, and maintained, but still not new.

Scarlett considered that maybe it was the lack of perfection that made the kitchen seem a homely place. She'd often struggled with the concept of homeliness. Her apartment was her home, and therefore should be thought of as homely, but she never felt that way, and now, in someone else's house, she did.

"Scarlett?"

She blinked and looked at Heather who was looking at her, obviously waiting for a reply.

"Sorry?"

"Mum asked if you wanted tea or coffee?" Heather repeated.

Scarlett looked at Sue apologetically. "I'm sorry, I was distracted. Water is fine."

Sue looked scandalised. "Water?"

"Mum, if she wants water—" Heather started.

"Of course, you can have water if you like," Sue said. "But we have a variety of teas. We have juice, we have milk, cola, cocoa, and sparkling water with raspberry."

"You have cocoa?" Scarlett asked in surprise. It was unusual to be offered cocoa, her favourite beverage.

Sue smiled. "Do I have cocoa? Come here."

Scarlett stood up and followed Sue into a large pantry. Sue pulled a light cord, and the shelves were illuminated by a single bulb that swung precariously over their heads.

The older woman pointed to the top shelf, where Scarlett saw at least eight different kinds of cocoa, including her preferred brand.

"Help yourself. It's usually only me that drinks it," Sue said, a friendly hand on Scarlett's arm. "I need the help to get through that little lot!"

"Thank you." Scarlett reached up and picked up a sachet of her favourite cocoa.

"Now, I make it with milk. How do you like it? Or do you want to make it yourself? Cocoa is a bit of a personal thing, isn't it?" Sue said, turning the light off again.

"It is," Scarlett agreed readily. "Would I be able to make it myself?"

"Of course. I know the feeling. No one can ever make it how I like it either."

Sue gave Scarlett the pick of the mugs from a large cupboard. For a house of supposedly only two people, there were an extraordinary number to choose from.

Scarlett picked the one that appeared to be the most usual in size and shape with industry standards to ensure heat management. She hated cold cocoa and would be able to judge the best speed at which to drink if she knew the mug resembled her own at home.

A few minutes later, she was sitting at the table again. Everyone had a drink, and Mike and Sue were discussing some of the rescue dogs who had recently come in, as well as their plans to redecorate the living room.

Heather coaxed them to not do anything too drastic and playfully nudged her father in the ribs as she reminded him of his age. Mike seemed very aware of his age but didn't seem to think that had anything to do with his ability to apply fresh wallpaper.

Scarlett watched in fascination as the family interacted with each other, and with her, as if it were the most natural thing in the world.

While she didn't feel completely relaxed, she didn't feel as stressed as she normally did when meeting new people. The Baileys were a kind and welcoming family, and Scarlett was very pleased that she had accepted Heather's offer to spend Saturday with them.

That didn't mean she didn't hold reservations about what the rest of the day would bring, but things were starting out surprisingly well.

29

Angus the Adorable Dachshund

HEATHER WATCHED as Scarlett and her mother walked a dog each along the footpath from the farm to the cliffs. She had her own dog, Monty, on the leash and had fallen behind while he did his business.

Her father and Angus, an adorable Dachshund that could easily have been rehomed but seemed to stay with her parents month after month, waited with her.

"She's a little young for you, isn't she, Pumpkin?" Mike asked with a playful grin on his face.

"Dad!" Heather admonished him. "There's nothing going on."

"I can tell. But the way you look at her…"

"Dad!" Heather repeated, swatting his arm to punctuate her message.

Mike laughed at her scandalised reaction. "How long has it been since you dated?"

Heather felt her cheeks heat up. "I'm not discussing that with you."

"Well, I'm going to guess it's since you and Aurelie went kaput."

Heather didn't say anything. She bent down and cleaned up Monty's mess, much preferring that task to talking to her father about her non-existent love life.

"I was just joking about the age thing. She's nice," Mike continued.

"She is," Heather agreed. She thought back to a couple of times over the course of the morning where Scarlett has said something that could have been considered rude or inconsiderate. Both times her parents had laughed it off, as was their way. "She can be a little difficult to talk to sometimes."

"Some eggs are harder to crack than others." Mike casually shrugged his shoulders. "She's a lovely young woman."

Heather realised in that moment that she was growing to think the same. Which was a little problematic as she had only intended to try to get through to Scarlett and show her that socialising with others wasn't all bad.

Instead she had demonstrated to *herself* how enjoyable she found Scarlett's company. Which was bad. And extremely unprofessional of her.

But she couldn't help it. It was happening no matter how unprofessional she knew it was.

"Her mother... stepmother... thinks she might be autistic," Heather said as they started walking again.

Mike looked at Heather as if she had recently come from another planet. "I think that's quite obvious, Pumpkin."

Heather chuckled. "Oh really? And what do you know about autism?"

"Pete, next door's boy, is autistic. Of course, there's all different kinds of autism. But Scarlett, well, she sees things differently, doesn't she?"

Heather looked up the track to where Scarlett and her mother walked side by side. Scarlett certainly did see things differently, sometimes more clearly than others and sometimes in a way that suggested she was completely confused by the world around her.

Those differences were a breath of fresh air to Heather. She really didn't have a clue what Scarlett would say next, and that was kind of exciting.

"You like her," Mike stated. "I can tell."

"I do not," Heather denied. "Besides, I can't. She's a member of staff."

Mike chuckled and shook his head.

"What's so funny?" Heather demanded.

"In one breath you tell me you don't like her; in the next you tell me why you can't like her. People who don't like people don't justify why they shouldn't in the very next sentence, Pumpkin."

Heather opened her mouth to argue but realised she didn't have much to say. He'd caught her out and she knew it.

"Come on, you two!" Sue called out.

Heather realised her mother and Scarlett had stopped in order to allow the two stragglers to catch up. They picked up the pace, and the four of them were soon walking together again.

"Scarlett, would you like to stay for dinner?" Sue asked.

Scarlett looked at Heather questioningly, waiting for an answer.

"Do you have other plans?" Heather asked, not wanting to push Scarlett in any particular direction. On one hand she knew Scarlett liked to eat alone; on the other she wanted her to feel welcome if she did wish to stay.

"No."

"What time is your train back?" Mike questioned.

"I have an open ticket," Scarlett said.

"Well, that's that settled. You'll stay for dinner," Sue said before turning and continuing her walk along the path.

Mike quickly joined her, grinning at Heather as he passed her.

Heather glared at him and then turned to Scarlett and whispered, "You don't have to if you don't want to. If you have to get back, or…"

"Or?" Scarlett asked.

"Or, well, anything…"

"Would you like me to stay?" Scarlett cocked her head to the side and regarded Heather curiously.

"I… would like that," Heather allowed. "If you want to?"

"Yes."

"Great."

"Heather, I don't understand why your parents are having difficulty rehoming Archie," Scarlett said seriously. "He is very well trained and would be considered very cute by most people. I would have thought that rehoming him would be simple, and yet they are struggling?"

"They want to keep him," Heather explained, watching her father scoop the small dog up off the ground and hold him like a baby in his arms.

"But they have both said that they have been unable to rehome him. Why not simply admit that they wish to keep him?"

"Because they don't want to admit that they are pushovers. When they set up the dog rescue, they made a promise that they would never adopt any of the dogs for themselves. They agreed that if they started to do that, they'd end up with far too many dogs."

"So, they are lying to each other?" Scarlett looked confused.

"No, they both know. They just haven't admitted it to themselves yet."

"They don't know?" Scarlett seemed stunned by the possibility.

"I don't know. Maybe, maybe not. Maybe they don't want to admit it to one another. It makes things real, when you admit to them."

"I don't understand people," Scarlett confessed.

"That's okay," Heather said.

"Is it?" Scarlett looked at her in surprise.

"Sure. People can be confusing, and we're all very different. It's not easy sometimes."

Scarlett seemed to take a moment to process this before she nodded. It appeared that the conversation was over.

"Come on, you two. So slow!" Mike called out over his shoulder.

Scarlett picked up her pace to catch up with Mike and Sue. Heather stopped and let out a sigh. Monty felt the lead stiffen and turned to look up at her curiously.

"I think I'm in trouble, Monty," she whispered. "I think I like her."

For the first time in living memory, Heather watched as her mother happily accepted a complete stranger into her kitchen.

Heather had been tasked with setting the table and was taking as long as possible to do so in order to watch the interesting scene taking place in the kitchen.

Scarlett had been adorned with her mother's second-best apron and was happily chopping and preparing items. Sue and Scarlett moved around the kitchen like a team who had been working together for years. Heather realised that it was probably because Scarlett exactly followed the instructions given to her.

As the day had progressed, Scarlett seemed to become more relaxed and even a little playful at times. She had even jested with Mike and his ridiculous dad jokes.

Heather was surprised how different Scarlett could be when she was away from work and relaxed. She suspected the relaxed part was the real key, as she'd seen Scarlett at Audrey's birthday party and that was nothing like the Scarlett she was seeing now.

Which meant that in all the time Scarlett had been

working at Silver Arches, she had never settled in. Never eased into a pattern as people so frequently did at their places of work.

"Pumpkin?" Mike called out from another room in the house.

"Coming!" Heather called back.

"It's amusing that he calls you that," Scarlett informed her.

"Hang around long enough and you'll get your own amusing nickname," Heather replied.

She exited the kitchen area to search out her father. It had only been a few hours, but her perception of Scarlett had completely changed. She felt closer to her and somehow understood her a little more.

There was still a mountain to climb before Heather fully decoded Scarlett's mysterious persona, but she looked forward to it as she now realised there was a lot hidden behind the supposed robotic exterior she had been warned about.

30

A Warm Hug at the End of The Day

SCARLETT COULDN'T BELIEVE how time had flown. Social engagements were usually long, laborious tasks that seemed to last forever. It wasn't unusual for Scarlett to feel utterly exhausted after even a short period of socialising, even with people she knew well.

For her to have spent most of the day with people she hardly knew and to feel relatively happy and safe was unexpected to say the least.

"You could stay the night," Sue suggested for the second time. "We have a spare room."

"Mum, she wants to go home. She doesn't have anything she needs to stay overnight," Heather gently nudged her mother.

"You'll come and visit again soon, won't you?" Mike asked.

Scarlett didn't know how to reply to that. Her invitations were extended through Heather, and she didn't know if she should expect another.

"Dad, don't pressure her," Heather said, pulling her coat on.

They were standing in the hallway to the farmhouse, preparing to say goodbye. Dinner had gone well, and afterwards they had retired to the living room to play a quiz game. To Scarlett's surprise, Heather was extremely good at general knowledge.

Luckily, Scarlett had a knack for remembering facts and figures and could hold her own. Mike and Sue were quickly knocked out of each round and both cheered Scarlett on in the hope she would end Heather's winning streak.

She hadn't, but Heather had admitted that Scarlett had given her a run for her money a couple of times.

Sue wrapped Scarlett in a warm hug. "It was absolutely lovely to meet you. I hope we see you again soon."

"Thank you, I had a good time," Scarlett said.

As soon as Sue had let her go, Mike was hugging her.

"Safe journey back," he said.

She wanted to comment that she had little control over the train, so it mattered very little how safe she was being. Instead she simply nodded.

Heather held the front door open for her, and they both left and got into the Jeep.

"Got everything?" Heather asked, starting the engine.

"Yes."

"Excellent, we'll be at the station in plenty of time for the twenty-past train."

They started to drive away, both waving to Mike and Sue who had come outside to see them off.

"I'm sorry that time ran away from us a bit," Heather said. "You'll be home rather late."

"That's not a problem. I have a book to keep me company." Scarlett patted her small rucksack.

"Oh, is it the one Nico lent you? The one I'm reading?"

Scarlett hesitated a moment. "No, I have moved on from that one."

"Ah." There was a long pause, and Scarlett got the feeling that Heather wanted to say something else. After a few moments, she spoke again. "You don't have to answer this, but is it because of the same-sex romance element?"

"I prefer non-fiction," Scarlett replied.

"I see. I'm sorry. I shouldn't have poked my nose in, I just know that some straight people don't enjoy reading lesbian fiction," Heather explained.

"I'm not straight," Scarlett corrected her assumption. "I do not see gender in the way many people do. I think I would be considered bisexual."

Scarlett didn't know if she was imagining things, but she felt the atmosphere in the vehicle change. Heather's fingers seemed to grip the steering wheel a little tighter, no doubt due to the narrow country lanes and the fading light.

"Oh, I see," Heather said. "So, you've been in a relation-ship with a woman?"

"Yes."

Scarlett looked out the side window, watching the sun set over the cliffs in the distance. It was easy to forget how beautiful the countryside was when one lived in the bustling city.

After a few minutes, they pulled up by the train

station.

"You still have a while before the train gets here, if you want to wait in the warm car?" Heather suggested.

Scarlett didn't mind either way but assumed, as Heather was suggesting it, that waiting in the car would be the most practical solution.

"Thank you."

"So, which book are you reading?" Heather asked.

"I'm reading about the Spanish Armada."

Heather smiled. "I see. Any particular reason?"

"It was on the shelf in the bookshop." Following two books from Nico that left a lot to be desired, Scarlett had decided to try a different genre. Not having many interests made picking a book very difficult. The book she had picked had an aesthetically pleasing cover and seemed a good size without being too heavy for her bag.

"And have you learnt anything interesting about the Armada?"

Scarlett quickly nodded. "I have. It seems the Armada wasn't as powerful as we are led to believe. A great deal of propaganda took place."

"Don't tell me; Elizabeth the First didn't really say that speech about her body being that of a weak and feeble woman but her heart and stomach being that of a king?"

Scarlett shook her head sombrely. "It's very unlikely. And Elizabeth's speech at Tilbury probably happened after the Armada had been vanquished."

Heather chuckled. "I'm not surprised. Disappointed, but not surprised. Still, it's a good message to send to young girls and women, whether it happened or not."

"I agree."

Silence loomed for a few moments, and Scarlett looked at her watch. She had a few more minutes to conduct small talk before she had to leave to catch her train. Not that she had to go far, the track being clearly visible from the Jeep.

"And you are reading the book Nico recommended?" Scarlett asked, not able to decide on another topic.

"I will, when I get some time. I haven't picked it up yet. I get the impression you didn't enjoy the book?" Heather asked.

"No, I didn't."

"As I'm about to read it myself, may I ask what you didn't like about it?"

Scarlett sucked in a quick breath. She didn't want to lie, but she wasn't entirely sure if she wanted to have this conversation with Heather either. The question presented her with little option but honesty.

"It made me sad."

"Sad?"

"Yes. Sad to see people having a relationship like that. A relationship that I'm unlikely to experience for myself," Scarlett explained.

Heather hesitated for a moment. "I'm sorry, I don't think I understand. What kind of relationship?"

Scarlett shifted a little uncomfortably in her seat. She considered her words carefully, knowing that she often struggled to explain what she was feeling with simple words.

"Love. True, all-encompassing love. I don't think I will ever experience that. The characters' actions are a mystery to me. The feeling of the love, as described in many romance books, feels alien to me. I don't appear to feel the way other people do. Therefore, love will probably never be something I truly experience." She shrugged her shoulder. "I believe I am incapable of it."

Heather sat up and looked intently at Scarlett. "I don't believe for one moment that you are incapable of love, Scarlett. And those books, they show a version of love that very few people will ever experience. They are a fantasy, a wish. Love isn't a one-size-fits-all kind of thing. It's different for different people. It isn't always fireworks and over-the-top emotions. Sometimes it's just a warm hug at the end of the day."

Heather placed her hand atop Scarlett's that sat in her lap. "You will experience love. I promise you that."

Scarlett didn't know what to answer to that, so she didn't.

They sat in silence for a few moments, neither speaking and both seemingly absorbed in the quiet. Scarlett distantly realised that Heather hadn't removed her hand, and Scarlett enjoyed the warmth and comfort it radiated.

Someone jogged in front of the Jeep, and both women looked up to see the train pulling into the station. Heather pulled her hand back.

"I should go," Scarlett said.

"Yes. I'll… I'll see you at work."

Scarlett opened the car door and paused. She turned back to look at Heather.

"Thank you for the day. I enjoyed myself."

Heather beamed at her, and Scarlett smiled back, satisfied that she'd said the right thing.

31

Being Cagey

Ravi saw Heather parking up in the Silver Arches employee car park and pulled up next to her. They stepped out of their respective vehicles at the same time.

"Good morning," Ravi greeted her happily.

"Morning," Heather said, getting her bag and suit jacket from her car.

"How was your long weekend?"

"Fine. Good. And you? Did you do anything nice?"

Ravi frowned. It wasn't like Heather to not have much to say after a visit to her parents. She usually spoke about ridiculous projects her father was working on, how many new dogs they had at the rescue, how nice it was to be out of the city.

"You're being cagey." He grinned. "What happened? What have I missed?"

Heather stopped walking towards the entrance and stared at him. She looked like she was going to deny the charge. Then she chuckled and shook her head. "How do you do that?"

"I know you very well," he explained.

She looked around the car park to check that they were alone and then took a small step closer to him. He lowered his head, eager to hear whatever gossip was about to be revealed.

"I invited Scarlett down to the farm on Saturday," Heather admitted.

Ravi was a little surprised by the admission. At first, Heather's interest in Scarlett had seemed purely professional, but Ravi hadn't been entirely sure that was all it was.

Scarlett was different to other employees at Silver Arches. Different because she was Scarlett and different because of who her father was.

Ravi had thought he'd detected a hint of non-work-related interest in Scarlett from Heather but had pushed it to one side, thinking it was his overactive imagination and his desire to see his friend in a relationship again.

But a trip to her parents' farm was definitely not a professional setting. Only a small handful of employees had ever been invited to meet Mike and Sue and spend time at the dog rescue.

It just wasn't something Heather usually did; she preferred to get away from work rather than bring it along with her.

"And how did that go?" Ravi fished.

"Well. Very well," Heather confessed, a touch of a smile on her lips. "She's very different out of work."

Ravi smiled widely. "Oh, is she?" he asked playfully.

That earned him a slap on the arm for being cheeky.

"Tell me everything," he requested.

"Not a lot to tell," Heather said. "We spoke, she stayed for dinner."

Ravi could tell by Heather's body language, grin, and tone that it was a lot more than that. Maybe nothing had actually happened, but he suspected that something had substantially shifted in their relationship.

He'd seen Heather act this way before, when she was interested in someone. And when she was in the early stages of falling in love. He felt happy for her. Not that he had any idea if they were a good match or not. He knew very little about Scarlett.

"So, what are you going to do next?" Ravi asked.

They'd just started walking again when Heather came to a second sudden halt. "Do?"

Ravi chuckled. "I don't know Scarlett well, but I am going to guess that she's not the kind of person to make the first move. Especially if there was any subtlety from your end in the way you feel about her. I doubt she would have picked up on it. Which means that is down to you."

Heather paled a little. "I... I hadn't actually planned to do anything. We had a nice time; I hadn't really planned much ahead of that."

"Do you want to have another nice time?" Ravi asked, trying to keep the suggestiveness out of his tone.

"Well, yes, maybe."

"That's kinda called dating, Heather," he told her.

Heather licked her lips. "I... I don't know if that's a good idea."

"Why not? There are no rules against employees dating. Hell, I've seen you set people up and then attend their weddings," Ravi reminded her. "You are *allowed* to date, you know."

"I know. I just… I don't know if it's appropriate," Heather admitted.

"Appropriate?" Ravi chuckled. "Why would it be considered inappropriate?"

They were suddenly illuminated by headlights.

"Because of that, for one," Heather said, looking at the new arrival.

Ravi turned around and looked at the expensive car pulling into the executive space. Leo Flynn had arrived, with no meetings booked in and no notice, as usual.

"Don't you want to call Leo 'daddy'?" Ravi asked.

Heather glared at him with such a strength that Ravi felt it in his soul.

"I'm only kidding," Ravi reassured her. "Look, Leo doesn't care about Scarlett; they're not close. I'm sure he won't care if you date her as long as she stays out of trouble. That seems to be his primary concern when it comes to her."

"Keep your voice down," Heather said through gritted teeth.

Leo was still in his car, far away, with the engine still on. There was no way he could hear a word they were saying.

Ravi grinned to himself. Heather had it bad. He was going to enjoy watching this play out.

32

Realisation

SCARLETT PLACED the book on the counter of the Gay Days pop-up shop and waited for Nico to come and serve her.

Nico, who was hanging heart-shaped lights from the ceiling of her temporary store, looked at the book and then at Scarlett's expression.

"Okay, I'm going to guess that you didn't enjoy this one either?"

"No, I did not."

"What was it you didn't like?" Nico asked.

Scarlett took in a breath. She'd confessed why she hadn't enjoyed the book to Heather a couple of days before and that had gone well; hopefully the same would happen with Nico.

"I find it… depressing that I will not experience that kind of love," she admitted. "Your lights are in breach of centre health and safety guidelines."

Nico looked at her lights and then at Scarlett. "What

203

are the odds of me convincing you to pretend you haven't seen these?"

Scarlett slowly raised an eyebrow.

"Fine," Nico grumbled as she started to remove the string of lights. "What do you mean by depressing? What kind of love do you think you won't experience?"

"The perfect kind. The kind that appears in these books, that appears from nowhere and is amazing in all ways."

Nico nodded. "Ah, yeah. I can see that. These books are all grand declarations of love, star-crossed lovers, all of that. If that's not your thing, fair enough."

Scarlett inclined her head, glad that Nico seemed to understand what she was saying.

"But remember that these books depict a grand romantic love that very few people will get to experience. It's escapism, attractive to the masses who daydream and believe that one day they could have the opportunity of being whisked off their feet by a beautiful billionaire who finds them irresistible."

"People find that extremely unlikely scenario… appealing?" Scarlett asked, confused.

"Oh yes. The idea that some rich, gorgeous someone wants you and will wine and dine you on their private yacht before they take you downstairs and show you how to tie a reef knot. Lots of people want that."

"But the probability of that happening is incredibly slim."

"Escapism," Nico repeated. "People don't read these books because they logically feel they are likely. It's a fantasy. A dream of a world better than the one they are in."

"Are there no realistic lesbian romance novels?"

"There are, but they don't sell as well. Nobody is really reading about two average people who bumble around until one of them asks the other to go to Pizza Express."

"Why Pizza Express?" Scarlett asked, wondering if that was a key component she was unaware of when it came to dating.

"It's the most romantic place in the world," Nico said with a wide grin on her face.

"Oh." Scarlett filed that information away for later.

"Bonjour. Are you Nico?"

Scarlett almost jumped at the presence of the woman who suddenly appeared beside her.

"That's me," Nico confirmed.

"I'm Aurelie. I'm here for your health and safety certificate. A copy is supposed to be in the file, but there isn't one."

"I've got it right here." Nico picked up a large folder and leafed through the paperwork. "I'm all about health and safety, me."

Scarlett watched as Nico kicked the string of heart-shaped lights under the table while looking for her certificate. She turned to look at the newcomer, trying not to stare. Aurelie was tall, impeccably dressed, beautiful, and presented herself with a confidence that Scarlett only dreamed of.

Moreover, Scarlett had never seen Aurelie before. She obviously worked for Silver Arches, but this was the first time Scarlett had seen her. Aurelie's gaze drifted to Scarlett and offered her a small wink and a smile.

Scarlett felt her cheeks flush and quickly looked away, focusing again on Nico.

Nico pulled out a sheet of paper from a plastic wallet and handed it to Aurelie.

"Thank you, this is perfect. May I take this to grab a copy? I'll bring it back in a few minutes," Aurelie asked.

"Sure, no problem." Nico giggled unflatteringly.

Aurelie grinned at them both and turned and left. Scarlett watched Nico lean over the counter to observe Aurelie's departure.

"Wow, she's hot," Nico commented. "I'm going to see if she's single when she gets back."

Scarlett raised her eyebrow. "How do you know she is a lesbian?"

"Gaydar." Nico finally stood up straight again once Aurelie was out of sight.

Scarlett didn't say anything, but she privately wondered if Nico's invisible powers were why she had offered Scarlett a lesbian romance book shortly after meeting her. Was Scarlett projecting some kind of signal that she was unaware of?

"Ravi!" Nico shouted.

Scarlett jumped.

"Ravi, come here!" Nico insisted.

Ravi was a great distance away but easily heard Nico and waved over to her to indicate that he was on his way.

"Ravi knows everyone," Nico explained to Scarlett. She waited anxiously for him to finish his conversation and join them, almost bouncing on her feet.

"Yes, Nico?" Ravi asked with a grin as he closed in on them. "You bellowed?"

"Who is the gorgeous French woman walking around like some Amazonian queen?" Nico got straight to the point.

"French? Health and safety woman?" Ravi confirmed. At Nico's nod, he continued. "That's Heather's ex. She's back from head office today."

For some reason a loud rushing in Scarlett's ears prevented her from hearing any more of the conversation. She was aware that Ravi and Nico were continuing to talk, but was unable to take any of their words in.

Ravi had casually informed Scarlett of some very interesting news; Heather dated women. Unfortunately, Heather dated women like Aurelie. Scarlett was all too aware that she was nothing like Aurelie.

Their conversation had only lasted a few seconds, but the class, elegance, confidence, and grace of Aurelie were all attributes that Scarlett knew she would never possess.

The rush of excitement that Heather dated women was dashed just as quickly by the knowledge of who she dated.

In the blur of emotions, Scarlett quickly became aware that she was interested in Heather, something that she hadn't been conscious of up until a few seconds before.

It wasn't unusual for Scarlett to not be fully aware of her feelings. It often felt like a large cloud sat atop her feelings like a heavy fog, preventing her from seeing or processing them. In a flash, that fog had cleared.

"Why did they break up?" Scarlett asked, breaking her

way back into the conversation with a question she simply had to know the answer to.

"Aurelie finished it," Ravi said. "But I think they just grew apart, too different. Anyway, if that was all, ladies? I need to get back to work."

Nico said farewell and Ravi left them to it.

Scarlett considered what she had just discovered. It was interesting, but she had no idea what to do with the information.

"Earth to Scarlett?" Nico said, waving her hand in front of Scarlett's eyes.

"I'm sorry, did you say something?" Scarlett asked, blinking.

Nico tilted her head to one side and regarded Scarlett. "Do you like Heather?"

Scarlett had no idea how Nico had come to that conclusion and wondered if it was akin to Nico's gaydar. Maybe she was giving off some kind of signal she was unaware of.

But she also appreciated Nico's honest and direct approach.

She nodded. "Yes."

"Can I give you some advice?" Nico pressed.

Scarlett nodded again.

"Don't hang around and wait for things to happen, especially when it comes to matters of the heart. If you want something, you should go out and get it. Before someone else does."

"Heather is interested in people like Aurelie," Scarlett pointed out.

"Heather and Aurelie broke up," Nico said.

"So, Heather wants to be with someone who exceeds Aurelie's assets. Assets which I don't have." Scarlett really didn't know why they were discussing the matter. It wasn't making her feel any better about herself to realise in the same moment that she liked Heather that she would never be enough for her.

"People aren't ranked on a ladder system, Scarlett," Nico said. "Aurelie isn't better than you. Yes, she's hot and French and tall and—"

"Is there a point to this?"

"You're all those things too," Nico said.

"I am not French. I'm half Irish."

Nico rubbed her face with her hand and looked suddenly tired. "Scarlett, you can't compare yourself to other people. You are you. You are beautifully unique. We all are. Embrace your differences, be proud of them. And if you want to ask Heather out, then you better go and do it. She might say no, and then you'll know where you stand, and you can get on with your life. But she might say yes."

"You think she might say yes?" Scarlett sought clarification.

"I think there's an extremely good chance that she'll say yes," Nico said. "But if you see an opportunity, then you have to grab it. How would you feel if someone else got there first? If Heather said yes to dinner with someone else tonight?"

"I wouldn't like it," Scarlett said, standing a little straighter and feeling a tad tense at the thought.

"Then do something about it," Nico suggested.

Scarlett nodded and spun around, leaving the pop-up

shop and heading for the offices as quickly as she could without running.

Saturday with Heather's family had been one of the most enjoyable social activities Scarlett could recall. It was certainly better than spending time with her own family and even better than some of the times she'd had with Steph. Especially towards the end when Steph had become cold and distant.

Scarlett mulled over Heather's last words to her. They had demonstrated an understanding that love came in many different forms and that even Scarlett could experience it.

She hadn't been able to shake the emotions she had felt in Hastings that Saturday. She couldn't explain exactly what they were, but there was a warmth there that she hadn't felt before.

Now it was becoming painfully clear that Heather was at the root of those feelings. Feelings that she wanted to experience again.

At first, she had been eager to keep Heather at arm's length, as she did with everyone else. Heather's insistence on joining her for lunch on those two occasions had frustrated her. Now, she felt she would love to see Heather sitting across from her.

Finding out that Heather dated women felt like a lottery win. Literally, considering the statistical probability of Scarlett being interested in that person and that person being gay.

But the stars had aligned and Scarlett fully intended to take Nico's advice and do something about it.

33

A Surprise Invitation

"IF THEY THINK they are getting a rent reduction, they have another thing coming," Leo said testily.

Heather wasn't going to question him on the matter. The large fashion chain was in financial difficulty and had requested assistance, but Leo had given a very firm no.

She'd just spent an hour in a meeting with him and the senior management of the store, an hour in which Leo basically reminded them that he wasn't a charity.

While Heather would have liked to have stood up for them, she knew when it was time to pick her battles. Such a large business would be able to take action in reducing the number of stores they had rather than shutting down completely.

She hadn't worked with Leo for long, but she knew that her influence over him was limited and she needed to ensure she stood up when it really mattered.

Leo continued to grumble about the meeting as they walked through the main thoroughfare of the centre.

Heather had tuned him out soon after they walked out of the meeting and into the public area.

She didn't want to have a business conversation where shoppers could hear them, and so she didn't reply to him and hoped he would tired himself out soon enough.

In her attempts to avoid talking to Leo, she was looking around the centre to check everything was in order. As usual, she checked on cleaning and maintenance standards, just in case anything had escaped the keen eyes of her team.

As she glanced around, her gaze rested on a familiar figure.

Her breath caught.

Aurelie was back.

Of course, she'd been expecting to see her ex, but she had hoped that she'd be able to avoid her a little longer. She thought it a touch unfair that she saw her the first morning Aurelie began working at Silver Arches.

"Father, may I talk to you?"

Heather was surprised to see an out-of-breath Scarlett suddenly appear at Leo's other side.

"Now is not a good time," Leo responded gruffly without even looking at her.

"I'd really like to speak with you now," Scarlett insisted.

"Fine. Make it quick." Leo didn't stop walking.

"Would you be averse to my dating someone?" Scarlett asked, keeping in step with Leo's stride.

That was enough to cause a reaction from him; he looked at his daughter with confusion.

"Why would I care?" he demanded.

Heather was torn between wanting to give them some privacy and desperately wanting to know whom Scarlett wanted to date.

It would be just her luck that weeks of her own inaction would pass only for Scarlett to find someone she was interested in dating at the very same time Heather realised that she'd quite like it to be her.

"Do whatever you like," Leo continued.

"Even if they are staff?" Scarlett sought clarification.

Heather felt faint. Who in Silver Arches did Scarlett want to date? She mentally ran through a list of all potential prospects. Surely Aurelie wouldn't act so quickly?

"Yes, I'm not a monster. As long as it doesn't interfere with work. Really, Scarlett, I don't have time for this," Leo said, picking up his pace a little in an obvious attempt to lose her.

"Thank you. Heather, would you like to go out to dinner tonight? I believe Pizza Express would be a good location?"

Leo and Heather came to a combined skidding halt. Scarlett continued walking a couple of steps before she realised that they had stopped. She walked back, looking at Heather curiously and clearly expecting an answer.

Heather felt a second set of eyes burning into her. Leo was glaring at her with shock and, quite possibly, some anger.

"Unless Pizza Express isn't a good location? I heard that it was?" Scarlett asked, clearly detecting that something was wrong but completely missing what it was.

"You're dating my daughter?" Leo asked Heather coldly.

Shoppers started to look at them, wondering why three members of staff were standing in the middle of the main walkway all looking at each other in various degrees of shock.

"Shall we take this somewhere more private?" Heather suggested.

34

Time Optimist

SCARLETT HAD no idea why Heather was dragging her and her father through a set of fire exit doors to a cold corridor but did as she was told.

The second the door clicked shut, Leo spun around to glare at Heather. "How long has this been going on?"

Heather held up her hands to calm him. "Nothing has been going on."

"You expect me to believe that?" Leo demanded, anger rising in his voice.

Scarlett realised then that she had mis-stepped.

It seemed that her father had lied to her, not that she could fathom why. He did care that she dated someone from the centre. And for some reason he cared a great deal that it was Heather.

"I expect you to believe me when I tell you that I'm telling you the truth," Heather said in a firm tone.

"I've made a mistake," Scarlett said, wishing she could take everything back. "I retract the question."

"Stay where you are," Heather ordered, causing Scarlett to pause halfway in her turn to leave. "I'd like to have dinner with you, Pizza Express or wherever."

Scarlett felt a rush of something in her stomach, possibly excitement, but it was quickly tempered by the realisation that her father was clenching and unclenching his fists.

She'd somehow upset him.

Heather took a position next to Scarlett and looked at Leo seriously.

"You need to learn to communicate properly with your daughter before you lose her," Heather told him. "Nothing has been going on between us. I invited Scarlett to see a dog rescue centre that my parents manage. We had a lovely day on Saturday, but nothing happened. That's not to say that it won't now. Scarlett is an exceptional woman, and I'm going to go on a date with her."

Scarlett felt her eyes widen. No one had stood up to her father like that before, certainly never for her.

"Don't you think you're a little old for her?" Leo asked, his voice seeming slightly calmer.

"Maybe. We'll find out for ourselves, I'm sure," Heather replied. "But I'm sure you don't need a blow-by-blow account of what we discover."

Leo looked a little pale and quickly shook his head. "No, no... of course not. I... well, I don't have much to say."

"Probably best," Heather said, her tone dripping with ice that even Scarlett could detect.

Leo's mobile phone rang. It was a sound that had long since been the final punctuation mark to any conversation Scarlett had had with her father.

He looked at the screen and then at the two women in front of him. "I have to go. You have my blessings, I suppose. Not that you need them."

"I should think not," Heather added.

"I… yes… I have to—" He turned and hurried through the fire exit door, back into the centre.

Once the door clicked shut, Scarlett looked expectantly at Heather, wondering what would come next.

Heather regarded her with a curious smile.

"Scarlett, why did you ask me out in front of your father?"

"I'd just been given some advice to not take too long," Scarlett explained. "Time was of the essence."

Heather chuckled. "I see. Well, in future maybe we could talk about things like that in private, just the two of us?"

Scarlett shrugged. "As you wish."

"What made you think time was such an issue?" Heather asked.

"I was speaking with Nico when Aurelie, your ex-girlfriend, came over. It occurred to me that there was a possibility that you might have wanted to rekindle your relationship with her. So, I wanted to ensure I asked you first."

Heather bit her lip and smiled softly at Scarlett. "I see. Well, let me just say that there's nothing between Aurelie and me anymore. There won't be any rekindling."

Scarlett felt a wave of relief at that news. She now realised that she had acted a little too quickly through fear that she may miss her opportunity. Fear that was entirely misplaced. However, the results were still as she desired.

"So, Pizza Express?" Heather asked, a smile lingering on her lips.

"Or another restaurant?" Scarlett added.

"Do you like Pizza Express?" Heather asked.

"No. I once ordered a salad, and it arrived with a piece of plastic from a pre-packaged salad bag in it." Scarlett winced at the memory.

"Then why did you suggest there?"

"Popular opinion indicated it was a good choice," Scarlett said, slightly glossing over the fact she had received intelligence from Nico that it was an extremely romantic locale.

"How about we meet at the food court and pick a place together?" Heather suggested.

Scarlett nodded.

"Six o'clock?" Heather added.

"No."

Heather grinned. "No?"

"No, I eat at six," Scarlett explained.

"Ten to six?" Heather asked.

Scarlett shook her head. She was beginning to realise that Heather's optimistic outlook on time would need to be factored into any future outings.

"Ten minutes for the kitchen to prepare the food, five minutes to choose from a menu and attract the attention of waitstaff, ten minutes to decide upon and walk to our chosen restaurant. Half past five would be practical."

"Five thirty it is," Heather agreed.

Scarlett nodded again. Details finalised, she turned and left.

35

Baby Girl

HEATHER WATCHED the fire door close behind Scarlett and chuckled to herself. Not even a goodbye. She'd need to talk to her about that.

Apparently, she'd have the chance that evening.

If someone had told her before Saturday that Scarlett Flynn would have asked her on a date, she'd have laughed in their face at the ridiculous idea. If they'd said she'd do it in front of Leo, she'd have thought they were crazy.

Heather was learning more and more that Scarlett wasn't like other people. She was unexpected, and sometimes inappropriate, but Heather found that that kept her on her toes. Not knowing what Scarlett would say or do next was turning into a bit of entertainment, even if sometimes it meant nearly having an argument with her new boss.

She exited the corridor into the centre and made her way back to her office.

She wondered what Leo was thinking. Was she about to be suddenly made redundant? He couldn't fire her for going on a date with his daughter, could he? And what did he care anyway? He wanted nothing to do with Scarlett.

When Leo had become angry, Heather had been determined to stand her ground. Scarlett's love life was nothing to do with him and his outrage was irrelevant. If he wanted to have a say in his daughter's life, then he needed to earn it.

In hindsight, she wondered if answering him back was such a good idea.

As she entered her outer office, Yasmin gave her a look that indicated that someone was in her office. Heather raised an eyebrow, and Yasmin mouthed Leo's name.

Heather sighed, took a deep breath, and walked into her office, closing the door behind her.

"Leo," she greeted him.

"Heather." He was standing in front of the window, looking a little unsettled and anxious.

"Are we going to have an argument?" she asked casually, taking a seat at her desk.

"No. No, I wanted to apologise," he said.

Heather hadn't expected that, but she wasn't about to let him off the hook so easily. "Well, that's nice to hear. But I thought I was too old for your daughter?"

"I didn't mean that. I mean, there is quite a gap between you. Well, I think there is. I don't know how old you—"

Heather glared at him, silencing him with a single look.

He swallowed and looked away, turning to look out of the window. Heather realised that he was nervous, something she'd never encountered before and hadn't expected.

"I..." He started and then stopped again. "It would be remiss of me if I didn't tell you, ask you, to... well... look after my baby girl."

Heather was very pleased that his back was to her as her eyebrows raised almost off her face.

Leo had never shown an ounce of care for Scarlett, and now he was attempting to make sure Heather looked after her. And referring to Scarlett as his baby girl, of all things.

"With respect, I'm surprised to hear that coming from you," Heather said, not willing to sugar-coat her surprise. "But I will, of course, look out for Scarlett's well-being. Whether we date or not."

He turned to regard her, a shameful expression on his face. "I'm sorry about my outburst. Scarlett can date whoever she pleases. If she finds happiness with someone, then that is wonderful news. Whoever that person is."

Heather leaned forward, clasping her hands together and placing them on the desk. "Leo, you can have a relationship with her, I'm certain of it. I don't know what happened to separate you both, but I can see that neither of you like it."

Leo rubbed his hand over his face. "I don't know. I think too much has happened. And I think we're too... different."

"You're her father. You obviously love her," Heather pointed out.

"I do. I really do."

Leo's phone rang. He glanced at the screen and sighed

before looking back at Heather. "Sorry, I need to go. Are we okay?"

Heather nodded firmly. "Absolutely. I'll catch up with you later."

He answered the call and left the office. The moment he was gone, Heather slumped back into her chair.

36

Baseless Optimism

RAVI SHOULDERED his satchel and picked up his jacket. He looked around the office to check he'd turned everything off before switching off the lights. He exited his office, closing the door behind him.

He'd made plans to meet up with the darts team after work. He wasn't much good at the game itself, but the company was worth embarrassing himself. As he walked along the corridors, he said good night to his co-workers and wished them a happy evening.

He exited into the public area of the centre and walked along the main corridor, taking a leaf out of Heather's book and checking that everything was in working order as he went.

He was surprised to see Scarlett standing nervously outside of the food court. It was the first time he has ever been able to clearly discern some emotion on her usually passive face.

"Scarlett?" he asked, detouring to check that she was okay.

She looked at him and offered him a tight smile. She shifted from foot to foot, and Ravi found it fascinating that something had got her so wound up.

"Is everything okay?"

"Why wouldn't it be?"

Ravi chuckled. "Well, you look a little worried, and you've just evaded a question. Which is pretty unlike you."

Scarlett looked pained for a moment, as if deciding whether or not to confess something. Ravi waited patiently, hoping to convince her that he could be trusted with his silence.

"I have a date."

Ravi grinned. "Oh, I see. Well, I'll leave you to it, then."

He knew the butterflies that proceeded a date and didn't want to bother Scarlett any further.

"Good night," he said, turning away.

"Wait."

He paused and looked at her. "Yes?"

If Scarlett had looked unsettled before, she now looked positively anxious.

"Do I… look okay?" she asked, seemingly almost annoyed at herself for asking the question at all.

Ravi swallowed down the chuckle that wanted to bubble up his throat.

"You look perfect, as you always do," he told her honestly. Scarlett was always neatly presented, never a hair out of place. "You seem nervous."

"I don't often date," Scarlett admitted.

Ravi could believe it. While Scarlett would be considered a beautiful woman by anyone who saw her, no one would argue that it was difficult to get to know her.

"I believe I will probably ruin it," Scarlett said, her honesty startling Ravi.

"If it's the right person, it will work out," Ravi told her.

"I disagree."

Ravi laughed. "Well, I disagree with your pessimism. Most things work out in the end. If it doesn't, then it's because there is something better around the corner."

"Do you actually find that baseless optimism helpful?" Scarlett asked.

Ravi laughed again, actually crying at Scarlett's words this time.

"The idea that if things aren't working out well then they will do soon is just a ludicrous platitude," Scarlett continued on calmly as if Ravi weren't dying of laughter in front of her.

Ravi wiped the tears from his eyes and regarded the young woman fondly. He was about to reply when he realised Heather had joined them, probably wondering what was happening.

"Heather, help me out here," Ravi said. "Scarlett doesn't believe me when I say that things will work out for the best in the end."

Heather looked from Ravi to Scarlett with a grin.

"Do you think that things won't work out for the best, Scarlett?" Heather asked.

"I believe the notion of accepting that things are 'not meant to be' if they do not work out is simply to protect the individual's feelings. It's like blaming a higher, invisible power rather one's own flaws, which are often the real reason why things do not work out."

Ravi chuckled at the cold, harsh honesty. "See? She's all out of optimism. Help me out, Heather."

"I think she's right," Heather admitted.

Ravi rolled his eyes playfully. "No! Not you as well!"

"But I think you're right too," Heather told him, patting his arm.

"We cannot both be right," Scarlett argued.

"You can," Heather disagreed. "You see, you're right, Scarlett: When people say that failed plans 'weren't meant to be' they are protecting someone's feelings. And that's because many people, though not all, are fragile when they come up against blow after blow. Losing job interviews, being turned down for competitions, not connecting with people, it can all be quite stressful for some, and so the belief that it 'wasn't meant to be' is comforting. It allows them some confidence to pick themselves up and try again."

"True," Ravi allowed. "We need to believe in something."

"Some of us do," Heather corrected softly.

Ravi realised that this was a teaching moment for Heather, who was trying to show Scarlett that people viewed things in different ways. She seemed to be pointing out to Scarlett that other people needed the comfort even if she didn't.

"I understand," Scarlett said.

"Great. We both won. I look forward to our next debate," Ravi told her with a bright smile. "Can I walk you out, Heather?"

"No, I'm having dinner here tonight," Heather said.

"Oh, what a coincidence," he said. "Scarlett has a date."

"I know." Heather looked at him meaningfully.

For at least five full seconds, Ravi wondered what on earth she was trying to convey to him. Then the penny dropped. His eyes widened, and he looked from one woman to the other with a growing smile.

"Right, I have a darts match to lose. Good night, ladies. Don't do anything I wouldn't do." Ravi turned on his heel.

Heather was clearly a faster worker than he had given her credit for. He smiled when he thought of Scarlett's adorably nervous display prior to their date; it seemed that love was in the air.

37

A Quiet Table

HEATHER WATCHED Ravi scuttle away and smiled before turning to face Scarlett. "Shall we?"

"Shall we what?" Scarlett asked.

"Find somewhere to eat," Heather clarified. "Do you have a preference?"

"No."

They walked into the food court, and Heather looked around the large, two-level space. There were fast food restaurants on the ground level and sit-down restaurants upstairs. Nearly every type of cuisine was available, and Heather had eaten in every single one of them multiple times.

Of course, she had her favourites, but she couldn't be seen frequenting one more than the rest.

Scarlett stood stiffly beside her, not offering a single suggestion.

"Do you like Chinese food?" Heather asked, deciding to get the ball rolling.

Scarlett tensed up ever so slightly. "Do you?"

"It's one of many cuisines I enjoy," Heather said diplomatically. She was trying to figure out if Scarlett was not a fan of Chinese food or was simply nervous about the situation as a whole. She'd need to go gently and search out any clues that Scarlett inadvertently dropped.

"Then we should have Chinese food," Scarlett said hesitantly.

"Scarlett," Heather said, trying to get the younger woman's direct attention. "I'm getting the impression you don't like Chinese food. Am I right?"

Scarlett shook her head. "I find it sometimes leaves me with an upset stomach."

Heather smiled, relieved that she was finally breaking through to her. The direct approach seemed to be one that worked; she filed that information away.

"Okay, then no Chinese food," Heather said, smiling to indicate that it wasn't an issue. "Tell me, where would you choose to eat if you were on your own?"

"I wouldn't. I'd go home."

Heather chuckled. "Pretend. You have to go out for dinner, just you. What would you be looking for?"

Scarlett looked around the noisy space and frowned, contemplating the question.

"Somewhere quiet," Scarlett confessed. "With simple food."

"That sounds like an excellent idea."

Scarlett turned to Heather. "But it should be your decision as well."

"And I'm perfectly happy with somewhere quiet and simple," Heather said. "I don't have a preference. I'm here for your company."

A light blush touched Scarlett's cheeks, and Heather felt proud that she had done the right thing.

"Benni's upstairs has a fairly broad, though plain, menu," Heather suggested. "And the restaurant has plenty of little nooks and crannies. We can find a nice, quiet table, if you like?"

Scarlett smiled, and Heather took that to mean she agreed. They walked to the escalators and went to the upper level. Heather took the opportunity to glance at Scarlett.

By default, Scarlett seemed to be quiet and reserved, but she also appeared to answer direct questions with honesty. Logically, that meant that Heather could get through to her by simply asking questions. It sounded obvious, but so much of Heather's social interaction included assumptions and silent communication.

That would need to change if she were to have any hope of a relationship with Scarlett.

A child started screaming as they so frequently did in shopping centres. The sound echoed around the food court, and Heather noted how Scarlett winced in clear discomfort.

Heather realised that the more she watched Scarlett, the more she was learning about the fascinating woman. Assumptions couldn't be made about what Scarlett thought or felt; Heather had to ask to be certain. That would take some getting used to.

At Benni's, Heather gestured to the large menu in front of the entrance.

"Check to make sure there is something you'd like to eat," Heather suggested. "I'll be back in a moment."

She walked into the restaurant and greeted the owner with a kiss on each cheek. Marco was like an old friend, and it had been a while since Heather had had the opportunity to see him.

"My date is looking at the menu," Heather said, wanting to be very clear as to the reason for her dining there. And to halt any potential comments about Scarlett. Heather was well aware that Scarlett had not exactly made friends throughout Silver Arches, and it wouldn't be a surprise if Scarlett had in some way offended Marco or someone else within Benni's at some point.

However, that wasn't Heather's problem at the moment. She was off work and looking forward to a nice meal and even nicer company.

Marco looked over at Scarlett and smiled; if he had anything to say he wisely chose not to.

"Can we have a nice, quiet table?" Heather asked.

"Absolutely. I can have Maddy seat you in the corner by the wine room?"

Heather knew the table in question; it was a booth towards the back of the restaurant and was very discreet.

Scarlett looked up from reading the menu, and Heather excused herself from Marco to join her.

"Find anything you like?" Heather asked.

"Yes, there are several dishes I could order," Scarlett said.

"Great, I have the perfect table for us."

They were led to their table, provided with menus, and soon their order was taken. Heather noticed a tension in Scarlett that she was determined to vanquish.

"How was work?" Heather asked.

"Adequate."

Heather smiled and mentally reminded herself that she needed to be more direct with Scarlett.

"Did you encounter anyone interesting today?"

Scarlett considered the question for a moment. "Mrs Shaw."

"Who is Mrs Shaw?"

"Mrs Shaw is an elderly lady with a habit of stealing socks from department stores and then pretending that she has lost her faculties when she is approached."

Heather sniggered. She hadn't heard about Mrs Shaw in particular, but she was aware that Silver Arches attracted a lot of interesting characters.

"Ah, is it always socks?" she asked.

"Yes. Often with animals on them," Scarlett explained.

"And did you approach her?"

"Yes."

"And how did that go?"

"She tried to tell me that the socks dropped into her bag. I had watched her on CCTV committing the crime. When I told her that, she asked if she was in the post office and if I was her granddaughter."

Heather laughed.

"Tara has informed me that we... let Mrs Shaw get away with it. Mainly because she is a terrible thief and gets caught every time. Also, because her infractions are reported to a social worker who works with Mrs Shaw."

"How do you feel about that?" Heather asked, knowing Scarlett had previously thought that criminals ought to be punished no matter who they were or what their crime was.

Scarlett offered a small shrug of her shoulder. "Mrs Shaw provides some variety to the other people I apprehend. She is not malicious, just misguided."

"What socks did she have this time?"

"Hedgehogs. They were strangely pink."

They regarded each other for a few moments before laughing.

Heather was pleased that conversation could flow easily with Scarlett as long as Heather pushed it along in the right direction. When conversation flowed, Scarlett seemed to relax.

Heather was beginning to understand that it really wasn't that difficult to change her behaviour to suit Scarlett.

In the past, she had given up her horror-movie fascination for a partner who couldn't stand the dark themes. She'd also stopped drinking milk in her coffee for a while for a partner who was lactose intolerant. Everyone bent to their partner in some way; it was natural.

It just happened that it was a little more difficult to correctly identify Scarlett's preferences on things.

Luckily, Heather loved a challenge.

"I was reading an article which described why many shopping malls have moved away from the retail and dining model," Scarlett explained as they walked through the upper area of Silver Arches. "Instead they are becoming leisure destinations. Roller coasters and flight simulators are becoming a frequent sight in overseas shopping centres, for example."

"That's true," Heather agreed. "But the British have always been a little different when it comes to shopping. While Arab countries, and America, like to expand what a shopping centre can be, most Brits do seem to want the traditional features of a shopping mall. One focused on shopping and dining."

"And yet, the layout of Silver Arches would be perfect for a roller coaster. I can see one being installed right down the middle of this walkway. A simple sixty-mile-per-hour launch would easily be accommodated right where we stand. I may speak to my father about it."

Heather stopped walking and blinked. Slowly and almost imperceptible, the corners of Scarlett's lips twitched.

"Are you messing with me?" Heather asked.

Scarlett couldn't control her facial expression any longer and smiled widely. "A little."

Heather laughed; she took hold of Scarlett's arm, and they continued their walk. Dinner had gone better than Heather could ever have imagined.

Once the initial nerves had dissipated and Heather had adapted her usual communication skills, things flowed as if they were old friends.

Scarlett relaxed in a way Heather hadn't even thought possible. Both women spoke at length about everything and anything that popped into Heather's mind.

Realising that the key to getting Scarlett to speak was to simply ask her a direct question, and often a follow-up or two, had opened the door to Scarlett's locked-away thoughts and feelings on a variety of topics.

Dinner came and went, and Heather had soon realised that they were monopolising a good table. She had also recognised Scarlett's discomfort at the growing noise from a restaurant that was becoming busy with the evening rush.

Her offer of a walk through Silver Arches was immediately accepted, and they had embarked on one of the slowest strolls through the upper level and towards the staff car park that Heather had ever taken.

It seemed that neither of them wanted to end the evening.

"While I joke about the roller coaster, I do feel a change of direction for Silver Arches would be prudent," Scarlett continued.

Heather couldn't agree more. While she loved the retail sector, it was in decline. People's habits had changed dramatically since the first shopping centres opened in the UK. Businesses needed to be nimble and quick to adapt, and that wasn't the case for many of the big-name brands who were struggling.

Silver Arches was essentially a building containing many businesses. If a number of those businesses were not profitable, then Silver Arches would suffer as a result. It was a familiar story up and down the country, with so many shopping centres either abandoned or becoming eyesores as they fell into disrepair.

"I agree," Heather said. "So, if not a roller coaster through the middle of the concourse, then what?"

Scarlett thought for a moment. "The events space on

the ground level could be turned into a series of seasonal experiences. It's my understanding that a dry ice rink is put there at Christmas time, as well as a Father Christmas meet-and-greet, but this could be expanded."

"Sounds interesting. How would you see that working?"

"A mixture of shopping, dining, and other experiences for guests, changing several times a year depending on the season, like Christmas, spring, Easter, summer, Halloween, and back to Christmas, as an example. We have the space to invite the local theatre companies to come and perform plays or musicals. Small stalls like the pop-up shops could easily be set up for stores of all sizes. The large retailers can select a small amount of seasonally appropriate products, and local crafts people can trade side by side with them. This would also allow contacts to be made between the two, perhaps allowing the smaller businesses to sell products to the larger businesses, which would be in everyone's interest."

"That sounds very interesting. Have you been thinking about this for long?" Heather asked.

"No. I just considered it now."

"Then you inherited your father's business acumen."

Scarlett stiffened at that. "I'm sure he would disagree."

"Well, it's a good thing that he isn't here," Heather said. "Because then I'd have to tell him that he's wrong."

Heather slid her hand into Scarlett's and squeezed it softly.

"Not many people do that," Scarlett said.

"I'm not like other people," Heather explained. "Sometimes people need to be told a thing even if it's obvious they won't like it."

"He listens to you. Respects you, I think."

"I respect him, too, in some ways. I can see he is a good businessman, but if I don't agree with him, I'll tell him so." Heather hesitated a moment before continuing. "I don't like seeing this obvious breakdown in your relationship with him. I know it's none of my business, and I'm probably projecting because I have such a close relationship with my own father."

Scarlett didn't say anything, and Heather realised she'd not directly asked a question.

"Would you like a relationship with your father?" Heather added belatedly.

"It's irrelevant," Scarlett replied. "We do not have one, and that is unlikely to change."

"But if it could, would that be something you'd be interested in?" Heather pressed.

Scarlett seemed to mull this over, and Heather waited. She had noticed that certain questions which required a little more thought certainly got it. Scarlett wasn't afraid to let her conversational partner wait while she considered a question from all angles.

"I found the relationship you have with your parents… fascinating. I almost felt like a part of it, despite only knowing them for a very brief period of time. I'd like to experience that. But I'm aware that that kind of relationship with my own father is impossible, so I don't think on it."

Heather opened her mouth to ask something else but

snapped it closed again. She was heading into territory that was most certainly not appropriate for a first date.

Her desire to see Leo and Scarlett reunited in any way needed to be slowed. She was aware that she didn't have all of the information. Leo had told her bits and pieces while Scarlett was like a vault on the subject. Heather had to accept that there may be just too many obstacles to overcome. Sometimes families were never going to be close.

"Maybe one day," Heather said, hopeful but noncommittal.

"Unlikely," Scarlett replied, honest as ever.

The loud, clattering sound of a security shutter being brought down on a nearby store made them both jump. The shops were starting to close.

"Closing time," Heather said, redundantly.

"Yes."

"Can I walk you to your car?"

"Ye—I'd like that," Scarlett said.

Heather smiled, noticing that Scarlett was at least making an effort to speak more.

They walked in comfortable silence through the centre and towards the quiet staff car park.

"I enjoyed this evening," Scarlett suddenly blurted out.

"So did I," Heather confirmed. "I'd love to do this again, if you're agreeable?"

Scarlett nodded quickly. "I'd like that."

Heather maintained a grip on Scarlett's hand as they walked across the car park. With Scarlett going from a supposed robot to one of the best dates she'd had in a long time, Heather couldn't believe how enjoyable the evening had been.

She distractedly wondered what Leo would think of them embarking on a second date, and maybe more. Then she thought of other staff members. Scarlett had made more enemies than friends, and now she was dating the boss. That wouldn't be well received.

Heather pushed such feelings to one side. That was something she would deal with as and when it became an issue.

Scarlett came to a stop by a Ford Focus. "This is me."

Heather didn't let go of Scarlett's hand. She found the connection comforting and wanted to maintain it for as long as possible.

Heather moved to stand in front of Scarlett, looking up at her and smiling.

"I had a great night," she said softly, hoping that maybe she'd be blessed with a good-night kiss.

"So did I." Scarlett didn't give much away.

"We'll do this again soon," Heather said.

"Are we going to kiss?" Scarlett asked.

Heather laughed. She leaned forward and placed her forehead on Scarlett's chest. Why was she trying for subtlety for this woman?

Heather swallowed the rest of her laughter and stood up straight again. Scarlett looked at her curiously, clearly still waiting for a reply.

"I'd very much like to kiss you," Heather admitted. "If you would like to?"

Scarlett nodded sharply and leaned down to capture Heather's lips. For some reason, Heather hadn't expected

Scarlett to react so quickly. Scarlett Flynn was definitely going to keep her on her toes.

She quickly responded but made sure to keep the kiss light and appropriate for a public workspace. It had been a long time since she had kissed someone, and her body awakened at the touch. For a brief second she was glad she was in a public space or the kiss might not have been as chaste. And that could lead to things that neither of them was ready for.

She ended the kiss and smiled softly at Scarlett. "Thank you for a lovely evening. I truly had a wonderful time."

"As did I."

"Have a safe journey home. We'll talk more soon to set something else up," Heather promised.

"When?" Scarlett asked.

"Sorry?"

"When will we talk more about a second date?"

Heather hadn't considered that and hesitated for a moment.

"Unless you are merely saying what you think I want to hear so we can end this encounter on a positive note?" Scarlett suggested. "If you didn't enjoy the evening, you can tell me now."

"No, not at all," Heather reassured her. "Scarlett, I'll promise you one thing; I'll always be honest with you."

Scarlett smiled tightly, her eyes searching Heather's, and Heather wondered if she was looking for an answer to her question or for any hint of a lie.

"I will text you this evening," Heather said. "And we will put a date in the diary then. Is that okay?"

"I would like that." Scarlett quickly leaned forward and placed a kiss on Heather's cheek.

She then turned and opened her car door.

"Good night," she said before she got into the car and slammed the door closed.

"Good night," Heather whispered in reply, smiling from ear to ear.

She watched as Scarlett started the car and then drove away without giving Heather a second glance as she left.

Heather dug her hands into her pockets and watched the red rear lights of the car until they were out of sight. Every time she turned a corner with Scarlett, she seemed to come up against a new mystery.

She found that fascinating and exciting.

Now she knew that Scarlett didn't do long or mushy goodbyes. She simply left. Scarlett liked certainty. Scarlett also liked to steal an extra kiss.

Heather couldn't help but chuckle to herself as she walked to her own car. She got her phone out and set herself a reminder to text Scarlett that evening. She had a suspicion that forgetting to do so would have serious ramifications.

She set another alarm to remind her to advise Scarlett of her forgetfulness. It was likely that she would forget something of great importance at some point, so the sooner she told Scarlett of that possibility, the better.

Honesty, she thought to herself. *It really is the key to all of this.*

38

An Exceptional Night

As HEATHER ENTERED HER APARTMENT, her phone beeped to indicate a text message had arrived. She looked at the message from Ravi asking how her night out had gone.

She smiled.

She locked the door, removed her coat, and put her bag on the sofa. Kicked off her shoes and flopped into the armchair. All the while, she considered what she was going to tell Ravi.

She typed in a couple of words and then deleted them before trying again. She paused and laid the phone down in her lap while she tried to focus her thoughts.

Pleasant thoughts had been floating through her mind all the way home, but now she had to distil and explain those thoughts to Ravi.

The night had been exceptional. There was simply no other word to describe it. Realising that nothing else would come to her any time soon, she sent that one word to Ravi.

She'd promised herself that she would go into the date

with no high expectations, but she'd ended the date hoping that something would come of it. She had a second date she needed to plan, which was a good start, but Heather's heart was already several steps ahead of that and planning for a fantasy future that she didn't know was even achievable.

Still, she knew it was nice to dream.

Even if Scarlett didn't apparently think so. The woman had explained, at length, that she didn't dream. Heather had argued that she probably did but was unaware of it, but Scarlett maintained that she didn't. And she absolutely didn't daydream.

True or not, Heather didn't know, but it was a fascinating insight and Heather was intrigued to find out more. If she was lucky enough to get that chance.

Spying her laptop on her coffee table, she picked it up and quickly opened a new blank email. She outlined the event plan Scarlett had come up with, explaining that the event space could be a cultural centre of sorts. A rotating series of events would keep the space new and fresh, and would enable them to engage with large and small shareholders as well as the local community.

She fleshed out the details a little and sent the email to Leo, asking for his opinion.

Her phone beeped, indicating that Ravi had replied. She glanced at the screen and chuckled at his disappointment with the lack of details.

Her reminder flashed up, telling her to text Scarlett and arrange a second date. She snatched the phone up, unlocked it, and quickly typed out a message to Scarlett.

It was mind-boggling to her that her memory was so

bad that she could forget about texting Scarlett while thinking endlessly about the woman.

Still, that was why her phone had so many reminders set throughout the day and evening.

She read through the message, asking Scarlett if she wanted to come over to her place for dinner one night, and then sent it.

While having access to Silver Arches and all it had to offer was nice, it was also nice to get away from work. She hoped Scarlett didn't think she was being too forward but assumed that Scarlett would immediately tell her if she was.

It was refreshing to be with someone who didn't have any walls or pretences. Scarlett was transparent and easy to understand once you figured out the best way to converse with her.

An icon moving on her laptop caught her attention, and she noticed that Leo had replied despite it being nearly eleven o'clock at night.

She opened the email and smiled to herself; he loved the idea and wanted to brainstorm it further to see how they could take the concept and make it into a full plan.

She replied, informing him that it was Scarlett's idea and that she would be putting her in the brainstorming group. She added that Scarlett probably had a lot of good business ideas and that they would both have to listen to her more in the future. Once she sent the message, she closed the lid of the laptop, as she didn't expect another reply from Leo that evening.

39

An Olive Branch

SCARLETT APPROACHED the Gay Days pop-up and placed the book on the counter. "I'm returning this, in line with our lending agreement."

"Did you love it?" Nico asked.

"No."

"Did you like it?"

"No."

Nico furrowed her brow. "Oh, I'm sorry to hear that. I honestly thought you would like this one. Do you want to try another, or do you think you are done?"

"I think I am done," Scarlett agreed. She had expected Nico to be more difficult to convince and had even prepared a series of statements to convince Nico to not try with a further book. Thankfully, that seemed unnecessary.

"Sometimes, and it pains me to say this," Nico said, "people just aren't bookish people. I mean, I still like you. I'll get over it."

Scarlett got the impression that Nico was teasing her and offered her a small, tight smile.

"Is that your dad?" Nico asked, gesturing over Scarlett's shoulder.

Scarlett turned around and spotted her father with a group of people she recognised from Intrex.

"Yes." Scarlett turned back to Nico.

"I looked him up online," Nico said.

"Why?"

"I was curious. He's investing in Silver Arches at a time when shopping centres are notoriously unprofitable. He must see something in them to be throwing so much money at it."

"And did your online research explain why he has invested in Silver Arches?" Scarlett asked.

"No. It told me more about him, though," Nico explained. "He has rarely put a foot wrong in the business world. Always turns a mess into a profit. Has a good eye for detail. That kind of thing."

"He has always been successful," Scarlett agreed.

"Do you two get on? I'm sensing not?"

"We do not get on. We haven't seen eye to eye for many years."

"Well, he's coming over, so maybe things are looking up?" Nico said, taking a step away to tidy some postcards which didn't need tidying.

"Scarlett, can we talk?"

She looked at her father and nodded.

Leo looked from Scarlett to Nico and then back. He gestured to a quieter area and Scarlett followed his lead.

"Heather told me of your ideas for rotating events in

the event space," he explained once they were alone. He took a breath and scratched his head. "I'd, um, I'd like you to be a part of the committee that organises it. I'll speak with your current line manager to split your duties, if that's okay with you?"

Scarlett stared at him in surprise.

"Well?" he asked, irritation becoming obvious even to her. "Do you want to be a part of it?"

"I would like that."

"Good, Heather said you would," Leo admitted.

A thought occurred to Scarlett. "Are you asking me to be on the committee because you want me to be, or because Heather has suggested it?"

He bristled. "Does it matter?"

"It does to me."

Leo maintained eye contact on a distant point beyond Scarlett's shoulder. "Fine. Heather pushed the issue and I agreed."

Disappointment flashed through Scarlett.

"Do you want the role or not?" Leo asked.

Scarlett considered the question. It was an interesting diversion from her current duties, yet it stung to know that her father didn't really want her to be a part of the committee.

"Forget it." Leo threw his hands up. "Forget I mentioned anything."

He stalked away and Scarlett watched him go. After a beat, she decided there was nothing else to be done about it and returned to work.

40

Consider It... Tracted

Yasmin entered Heather's office with a takeaway coffee mug. Heather looked up and smiled happily.

"You're a lifesaver."

"Scarlett Flynn is outside, and she wonders if you have some time. But she wants me to highlight that it is not an important matter if you are busy," Yasmin said, obviously repeating Scarlett's instructions verbatim.

Heather chuckled. "Send her in."

Yasmin grinned before leaving the office and advising Scarlett that she could go through.

Heather leaned back in her chair and took a sip of her coffee. The day was looking up; she had coffee and her new love interest was romantically visiting her in the middle of the day. What could be better?

Scarlett entered the room and stood to attention in front of Heather's desk.

"I want you to stop speaking with my father about me," Scarlett announced.

Heather raised an eyebrow. "Can't do that. He's my

boss, you're my employee. Sometimes there will be crossover."

Scarlett looked aggrieved, and Heather gestured to the chair in front of her desk. Scarlett sat down while Heather got up and closed the office door that Scarlett had left wide open in her hurry to come in and say her piece.

While Heather had full faith in Yasmin, she didn't want to be overheard during a conversation that may well turn personal.

She perched herself on the corner of her desk and looked down at Scarlett. The young woman was clearly distressed, and Heather bet she had an idea why.

"Can I ask what brought this on?"

"You interfered with my relationship with my father."

"No, I told my boss that I thought you would be a good candidate to be on a committee for a project that you suggested to me just last night," Heather corrected.

"He said you pushed the issue."

"I did," Heather confessed. "I told him that you needed to be on the committee, and he argued that you didn't. And then I argued that you did. We went around a few times on that topic."

Heather stood, walked around her desk, and sat back down again. She waited. For a change, she was going to make Scarlett come to her.

Scarlett looked at her with confusion. "What was the result?" she finally asked.

"He agreed with me. But I didn't push the issue because you are his daughter; I pushed the issue because you came up with the idea and I firmly believe that you have skills that would lend themselves to the project."

Heather sipped her coffee. "I may push your father now and then, but I can't change his opinion once his mind is made up. He's a stubborn man."

"That is true." Scarlett's expression softened. "I'm sorry, I shouldn't have come here."

Heather smiled. "I'm glad to see you, even if it is to correct a misunderstanding. Are you going to be on the committee?"

Scarlett shook her head. "No, he retracted the offer."

Heather blinked. "What happened?"

"He offered me the role. I asked if he wanted me on the committee or if he was merely asking because you had suggested it. He said you pushed the issue with him and asked again if I wanted the role. While I was considering it, he retracted the offer."

Heather rolled her eyes and let out a sigh. It was one step forward and three steps back with father and daughter.

"Did you want to be on the committee?" Heather asked.

Scarlett nodded. "I believe so."

"Fine, then you're on it."

"The offer was retracted."

"Consider it… tracted. Whatever." Heather rubbed her forehead wearily. It had been a trying morning, and now she was walking the tightrope between Leo and Scarlett with little luck.

"I'm sorry," Scarlett repeated.

"You don't need to be sorry."

"I'm causing you problems."

"You're not," Heather reassured her. "In fact, seeing

you enter my office just now caused me to smile for the first time today. Until you told me off." She winked.

Scarlett offered a shy smile. "I am still invited to your apartment for dinner this evening?"

Heather nodded. "I'd like that a lot."

The evening before, Scarlett had quickly replied to Heather's text and admitted that she was eager to see her again soon. The boost to Heather's ego and subsequent rush of nerves and adrenaline meant that sleep had taken a while to come.

"Scarlett, I need you to know that I will probably continue to try to bring you and your father closer together. It's in my nature to try to fix things, especially when it comes to family. If I overstep, I apologise now, and I know you'll tell me. But please know that if I do overstep, I mean well. I don't want to hurt you."

Scarlett nodded.

Heather waited a beat to see if she was going to say anything, but as the silence dragged on, it became clear that she wasn't.

"Are we finished with this meeting?" Scarlett asked.

"I suppose we are," Heather agreed. "I'll see you tonight."

Scarlett nodded and left the room. Heather watched her go and smiled crookedly. She still needed to have that conversation regarding other ways to say goodbye.

Although watching Scarlett breeze out of a room as she pleased was rather amusing.

41

Networking

"How's business?" Ravi asked Nico as he approached the pop-up shop. He'd seen a steady stream of customers at the temporary store since it had been open, but he wasn't sure if they were browsers or buyers.

"Pretty good. I'm getting your posh shopping centre folks on board with good books." She gestured her head towards the large chain bookstore across the way. "Still more people going in there than coming over here. You should have put my pop-up outside their front door."

Ravi laughed. "I don't think they would have liked that much. There's talk of us running these more often. Would you be interested in coming back in the future if we did?"

"Absolutely," Nico enthused. "Sales are good, and there's so many people to watch. It gets quiet in my little store."

Ravi grinned and leaned on the pop-up counter and looked around. "What kind of people-watching do you get up to?"

Nico approached and lowered her voice to a whisper. "There's this old woman who steals socks; she's quite a laugh. Then there's this man, I think he works in IT, who is clearly madly in love with the redhead who works in the jeweller's. She's obviously into her manager, who is married. But my favourite is the young guy who works at the hot dog place."

"What's his story?" Ravi asked.

"Excuse me, Mr Flynn?" Nico suddenly called out, nearly deafening Ravi in the process.

Leo Flynn had been walking past and came to a stop, regarding Nico with a curious expression. He came over.

"Yes?"

"Hi, I'm Nico. I just wanted to thank you personally for allowing all us independent shopkeepers to set up these pop-ups in Silver Arches. It's made a real difference to us."

Leo looked a little surprised at the thanks but quickly recovered. "You're most welcome."

He smiled happily, despite having nothing whatsoever to do with the project. Ravi kept his mouth closed.

Nico flashed Leo a bright smile as an end to the conversation. Leo returned the smile and went on his way.

"What was that about?" Ravi asked.

"I'm networking."

"You're sucking up," Ravi pointed out.

"Look, do you want to know about Hot Dog Boy or not?" Nico asked.

Ravi knew that Nico probably had a reason for introducing herself to Leo and surmised that he'd find out more about that in due course. Meanwhile, the story of the guy who worked at the hot dog stand seemed like it would be a good one.

"Okay, go on, what about Hot Dog Boy?" Ravi asked.

42

Centre Guidelines

HEATHER KNOCKED on the door to the security office and stepped inside. A few people looked up at her and smiled their greeting, Scarlett being one of them.

Heather was five minutes early in order to do a very important piece of housekeeping. While the staff at Silver Arches were as tight knit as a family, they also gossiped like one.

She'd come to the decision that she needed to be open and honest about the fact she was seeing Scarlett from the start. There would still be gossip, but at least she wouldn't look like she was actively trying to hide anything.

Heading straight for Tara's office, she knocked on the frame of the open door before stepping in.

"Afternoon," Tara greeted her, a cocky smile on her face.

She knows, Heather thought.

"Hi." Heather closed the door behind her and came farther into the room, leaning on the back of the chair in front of Tara's desk.

"To what do I owe the pleasure?" Tara asked, leaning back in her chair and still grinning from ear to ear.

"I've come to advise you of a change in situation between Scarlett and myself," Heather explained, even though she felt Tara already somehow knew about that private matter.

"Oh really?" Tara asked, sounding utterly unsurprised. "Are you asking for my permission to date one of my officers?"

Heather rolled her eyes at the jesting. "She told you?"

"She did. In accordance with centre guidelines," Tara explained. "Chapter fourteen, section three, paragraph two, if my memory serves. Something about the possibility of a relationship potentially hindering centre operations."

Heather pinched the bridge of her nose. She'd been meaning to speak to Tara all day, but clearly her delay had allowed Scarlett to get there first.

"I give you my blessing," Tara said grandly, smothering a chuckle.

Heather rolled her eyes. "You're enjoying this far too much."

"I am!" Tara agreed. "You should have been here when she stood on a chair and announced it to the whole team during our lunchtime meeting."

Heather's eyes widened. "What?"

Tara started to laugh. "It was a thing to behold. But, seriously, no one is bothered. You two just go and have fun. I'm happy to see you happy. Well, you were happy when you stepped in; now you're horrified."

"Not horrified, just wishing I had spoken to her before

she spoke to you. All of you," Heather said. "What did she say?"

"Simply reassuring us all that while you two may be dating, it wouldn't prevent her from upholding centre guidelines. A reassurance that she isn't breaking them either. No juicy details, and I really did try to get them out of her." Tara was almost crying with laughter at this point.

Heather sighed as she watched Tara lose herself over the situation. "Are you almost done?"

"I'm sorry." Tara wiped at her tears. "Sorry. It was just so good. I wish you'd been here. You would have died. Or thrown yourself at her to get her off the chair. But, in all seriousness, everyone will be happy for you."

"I hope so," Heather said softly.

Tara sobered up immediately. "They will. Scarlett has made some enemies, but that will all be forgotten in time. She's actually getting better at integrating with people lately. And people love to see a romance blossoming."

"Let's hope so. I already have Leo to contend with; I don't need the team turning against me," Heather admitted.

"They won't," Tara said determinedly. "You have the respect of everyone at Silver Arches; that's not going to change. And Scarlett is entertaining as hell. I look forward to her next public broadcast."

Heather narrowed her eyes and stared at her.

Tara tried and failed to swallow another chuckle.

43

Small

Scarlett pulled up in the visitor's space and applied the handbrake. So far, the second date was going well.

Heather had met her in the security office for their date. Following a meeting with Tara, where laughter could be heard in the outer office, Heather emerged and asked Scarlett if she was ready to go.

Scarlett was grateful that Heather seemed to understand her desire to eat at a similar time each day. Due to the time their shift ended, it would have been impossible to get to Heather's apartment and then start cooking a meal. Considering this in advance, Heather had suggested they pick up takeaway from the food court before heading to her place.

The fact that she had pondered the matter and come up with a plan that was suitable had cheered Scarlett immensely. Before Heather told her the plan, Scarlett had been wondering how to bring up her desire to eat at precisely six o'clock and the issues that might bring.

Once the food had been collected, they each got into

their respective cars and drove to Heather's apartment. Heather had offered Scarlett a lift, but that would have left her own vehicle at the centre, which would have been inconvenient.

Scarlett got out of the car and looked up at the modern apartment building. It looked pleasant; residents had made an effort to decorate their balconies without going overboard. Elegant flower boxes and the odd piece of garden furniture made the building look homely.

She joined Heather, and they entered the communal lobby and got the lift to the top floor. Heather handed Scarlett the bag of food while she got her keys out and let them both into her apartment.

Scarlett stepped in and looked around in fascination. "It's very small."

Heather laughed. "Well, it's the right size for me."

"That's true," Scarlett agreed.

"I'll get some plates." Heather took the food from Scarlett and entered the kitchen.

Scarlett followed, looking around at the compact kitchen with its small dining table in front of a window that overlooked a beautiful garden down below.

"Some people might be offended if you go around calling their living space small," Heather pointed out as she plated up food.

"But it is small," Scarlett explained.

"It is, but some people may not like you mentioning it. Maybe use a word like... cosy?"

"What if it doesn't feel cosy?" Scarlett asked.

Heather paused. "You know what, I shouldn't be telling you what to say. I'm sorry, that was rude of me."

"It wasn't rude," Scarlett disagreed. "You simply made a suggestion."

Heather placed the two plates of food on the table. "Should I really be correcting what you say and how you say it, though? And can I get you a drink?"

"Water," Scarlett said. "And yes, if I have said something that could be considered rude. I know I... rub people the wrong way. Frequently."

Scarlett sat down, and Heather placed a glass of water in front of her and handed her some cutlery.

"Do you know why that is?" Heather asked.

"I doubt it has escaped your notice that I'm different to most people," Scarlett said.

She knew that Heather was perceptive and intelligent; there was very little possibility that Scarlett's different behaviours had alluded her.

"It hasn't escaped my notice," Heather confirmed, pouring herself a glass of wine. "Do you know why that is?"

"Presumably I'm autistic," Scarlett replied.

44

Different, Not Weird

Heather stared at Scarlett in shock. She'd been hoping that they could slip into a conversation about Scarlett's behaviours and maybe figure out a way to talk about them in more detail.

But here was Scarlett, surprising as ever, just coming out and saying the thing that had been resting on Heather's mind.

"You're autistic?" Heather asked.

"I believe so," Scarlett said, picking up a fork and separating the different elements of her meal on the plate. "I exhibit many of the symptoms."

"I see." Heather put the wine bottle back on the counter and took her seat opposite Scarlett. "I had considered it a possibility, but I didn't know whether you knew or not."

Scarlett looked up at Heather with a kind expression that still loudly indicated she thought Heather might be stupid.

"I've lived my life for twenty-six years. I noticed that I

was different from other people when I was as young as five. It became more obvious as I got older. How would I not know?"

Heather didn't have an answer for that. Perhaps it had been a stupid question.

"But you've never been diagnosed?" Heather guessed.

"No. I considered it, but never got much further than that. I didn't know if there was much point. As I say, it's quite obvious to me." Scarlett finished separating her different foodstuffs and then regarded Heather seriously. "Will that be a problem for you?"

"No," Heather said. "But it does mean we have to give each other a little more leeway. I've never dated someone with autism before, so I don't know what you need from me. I might make mistakes; if I do, then you have to tell me."

Scarlett frowned and then returned to her meal.

Heather smiled. "Like that, you just frowned. Why?"

Scarlett looked back up again. "I'm just surprised. I'm used to being the one who makes mistakes and has to adjust my behaviour accordingly."

"I'm not an expert, but I thought autism meant that sometimes those behaviours are beyond your control?" Heather asked.

"Some do seem very difficult to change," Scarlett confessed. "But in previous relationships, like my last one, I felt as though I was the one at fault."

Heather frowned. She didn't like the idea of that at all. She still had a huge amount to learn about autism, and specifically about Scarlett's autistic behaviours, but she was aware that adapting to those would often have to come from her end and not Scarlett's.

The fact that Scarlett had been in a relationship where that wasn't the case was unsettling.

Heather pointed to Scarlett's plate of Indian food with her fork. "You seem to have issues with food. Can you tell me more about them?"

Scarlett looked down at her plate. "I do not like food types to mix."

"I see. How about… pizza? That's many ingredients on a piece of dough. How do you feel about that?"

"I like pizza. Pizza is a meal; the different ingredients are meant to be there. But this chicken korma, for example, the rice, the naan, and the korma itself are all separate entities. I wouldn't like them to touch." Scarlett ducked her head shamefully. "I know that is 'weird'."

Heather put her fork down and leaned over the table to place a finger under Scarlett's chin and encourage her to look up again.

"It's not weird. It's different. It's you. If you don't want your korma to touch your rice, then that's absolutely fine. And now I understand that and I can make allowances for it."

"Should you have to?" Scarlett asked, eyes beseeching.

"I want to." Heather removed her finger and took a sip of wine. "Being with someone means making choices to make them feel more comfortable. In the same way that I may want to do something nice for you, like bring you your favourite slippers on a cold winter's night."

Scarlett inclined her head, and they ate in comfortable silence for a few moments.

"Scarlett, I have to admit, I hate the smell of lavender. It reminds me of my grandmother's house when she died. I'd appreciate it if you could not wear lavender scents," Heather said.

Scarlett looked up at her and narrowed her eyes. "You're coming up with things I can do to accommodate your... idiosyncrasies."

"Yes."

"Why?"

"To demonstrate that we all have them. If you cannot wear lavender scents for me, then I can make sure your food doesn't touch while we eat it at six o'clock for you."

Scarlett considered this for a few beats before saying thank you in a tone so soft that Heather nearly missed it.

"Anyway, how was your day?" Heather asked.

"Average," Scarlett replied. "But I have a story to tell you about a suspected thief I was shadowing."

Heather smiled widely. It was the first time that Scarlett had offered up information on her day without being asked. It was a small step, but an important one nonetheless.

45

A Purpose

SCARLETT SIPPED THE COCOA. Heather had apparently stocked up on Scarlett's favourite brand at some point. It was a small gesture but a hugely appreciated one.

They were sitting on a small sofa in Heather's apartment, having had a similarly successful date to their first one the previous evening.

After a small hesitation that came when Scarlett confessed her autism suspicions, things had quickly got back on track.

They spoke about their respective days, about work, about travel, about hobbies. Scarlett found it easy to talk to Heather, as she never had to wonder what was appropriate and what wasn't. Heather guided the conversation most of the time. The few occasions when Scarlett attempted to do so, Heather easily slipped into whatever conversation Scarlett had decided on.

It was unlike other social interactions she had experienced; it was easy.

"Can I ask why you left the army?" Heather asked, sipping from her second glass of red wine of the evening.

Scarlett made a note to get some red wine for her own apartment, in case things went well and they continued to see each other.

"I was asked to."

Heather chuckled. "Well, I gathered that much. But why did they ask you to leave?"

Scarlett put her mug of cocoa down on the coaster on the coffee table. "I sometimes questioned orders."

"Did you now?" Heather asked, in a tone that Scarlett assumed was sarcastic.

"I did. Sometimes I was given different orders from different people. And sometimes those orders were not the same as ones we had received in our training."

"And you pointed that out, upset people, got moved to another team, department, et cetera, until they ran out of places to move you?" Heather accurately guessed.

"Exactly."

"Do you miss it?"

"I miss the purpose of it," Scarlett admitted.

"Do you not feel that you have a purpose at Silver Arches?"

"I have a job, but I feel that I've been placed some-where that I can fulfil a goal while causing the least disruption. In the army, I was part of an enormous organ-isation that exists to serve the country."

"Now you stop Mrs Shaw from stealing socks," Heather said, understanding obvious in her voice.

"A worthy task, but not a lifelong purpose," Scarlett said.

"Then you need to find a new purpose, something that fits with your beliefs, your passions, and your skills." Heather sipped some wine. "If you want to, of course."

"Like the firefighter in *Burning Passion*," Scarlett pointed out.

Heather looked confused.

"The first book Nico loaned to me," Scarlett explained. "The firefighter is injured in a fire, unable to go back to work. She felt being a firefighter was the only role she could do and became depressed. A new lover convinced her to follow her dreams of becoming the small business owner of an adventure travel company…"

Scarlett paused and cocked her head to one side. "I hadn't realised that the book had taught me a lesson, but now I think it did. I owe Nico an apology."

"She does seem to believe she has a sixth sense for providing the right book to the right person at the right time," Heather agreed. "So, are you going to open an adventure travel company?"

Scarlett chuckled. "No. I don't think that is my passion. I had considered opening a business with my ex-girlfriend. We had planned to open a furniture shop when we left the army."

"What kind of furniture?" Heather asked.

"Upcycled furniture. Finding furniture that was no longer of use to people and renovating it or making it into something else. Steph enjoyed those kinds of projects."

"Did you?"

Scarlett considered the question for a few moments. "Not particularly. The fumes of the glue and the paint were bothersome."

"So, more Steph's passion than your own?" Heather suggested.

"Yes."

"Is that why you broke up?" Heather asked.

"No. Steph ended things with me because I am too much hard work to be with. She told me that I am too weird, and she couldn't fix me."

Heather stared in surprise. "I'm sorry?"

Scarlett felt as if she had done something wrong and hesitated a moment before repeating what she had said.

"She told you that?" Heather clarified.

"Yes."

Heather put her wine glass down on the coffee table with a small thud before standing up and pacing around the small living space.

Scarlett watched her, frowning as she wondered what had agitated the woman so.

"She actually said that to you? Actually called you weird? To your face?"

"I am weird," Scarlett said.

"No. No, I'm not going to accept that. You do see things differently, but you are not weird and you most certainly do not need to be *fixed*. To say that to you is… well, it's cruel." Heather continued to pace, shaking her head as she went.

A small beat of happiness rushed through Scarlett. Steph's words had rung in her ears for a long time, cold and hurtful. But Scarlett had always believed that they were deserved. Heather's reaction indicated that perhaps Scarlett was right for feeling so wounded by Steph's words and behaviour.

"Scarlett, you're not hard work. And there is nothing to be fixed." Heather stopped pacing and looked at her seriously. "You know that, right?"

Scarlett didn't know that at all. She had for a long time thought that Steph's words were accurate and a reflection on what most people probably thought.

Although she hadn't verbally replied, she assumed her answer must have been written in her expression. Heather sat on the arm of the sofa next to her and pulled her into a hug.

"I'm sorry she said that to you," Heather whispered into her hair. "I'm even more sorry that you think there's a grain of truth to that statement."

Scarlett wrapped her arms around Heather and rested her head on her shoulder.

She never thought she would have someone in her life who seemed to so thoroughly understand her, or at least to be determined to try to. Heather Bailey was someone that Scarlett didn't think could possibly exist; she was exactly what she needed. She just hoped that she could repay the favour.

"What is your passion?" Scarlett asked.

"The centre," Heather said without hesitation.

"You're very lucky."

Heather released Scarlett from the hug and looked at her meaningfully.

"I am," she said before ducking down and kissing her.

46

A Busy Morning

HEATHER ARRIVED at work the next morning bright and early. Sleep had eluded her the previous evening despite her exhaustion.

Scarlett had stayed until one in the morning. They'd talked about so many subjects that Heather had lost count. They hugged, they tentatively kissed, they shared stolen glances and smiles.

It wasn't a date like any Heather had experienced in the past. But it was also more than she could ever have hoped for.

Dating someone so inherently honest and open had meant the second date had in many ways felt like a tenth date. She felt as though she knew Scarlett better than she did some of her close friends.

If she wondered how Scarlett felt about something, all she needed to do was ask. The freedom of that was astounding.

And the realisation that Scarlett was very much aware of her probable autism was another eye-opener. With that elephant in the room acknowledged, they could talk even more openly about things.

But they'd balanced the big stuff with the smaller matters, and sometimes big and small rolled into one. At one point, Scarlett spoke about a childhood Christmas and a particular popular toy she had been given by her father. That had forced Heather to recognise the not-insubstantial age difference between them.

That had been a matter for discussion too. While Heather felt it was something that may cause issues, Scarlett had disagreed. They'd eventually decided to wait and see what happened, which was essentially how most relationships worked regardless of the ages involved.

Heather got out of the car and headed towards the centre's entrance, fiddling with the clasp on her bag as she walked.

"Hello, Heather."

The familiar French voice was the last thing Heather wanted to hear first thing in the morning. Before her morning coffee, no less.

"Aurelie," she greeted the woman.

She looked up to see her ex standing before her, as flawless as ever. It looked like she had been waiting for her arrival.

"You've been avoiding me," Aurelie said.

"I have," Heather agreed. "I didn't think there was much to be said."

"I wanted to explain why I came back here. I don't want to cause any issues for you. Or any distress for either of us."

Heather stood tall and jutted her chin up defensively.

This woman had hurt her, badly. She wished she could be mature enough to act as if she didn't care, but she did care. The wounds were still raw.

"Why are you back?" Heather asked.

"I want a promotion, but to get it I need certain experience. Experience I can't earn at the head office. I'm back to get that quota, to show that I can do the job."

Heather felt relieved. This wasn't a scheme to get back at her, or a permanent arrangement. As centre director she made a lot of staffing decisions, but some of those still came from The Arches Group directly, and Aurelie's appointment was such a one. Heather could technically make a complaint, but she never would. And now she wouldn't need to.

"I understand," she said.

"I don't want things to be awkward," Aurelie said. "I know that's easier said than done."

"It is. I... I don't want there to be awkwardness either. Which is why I avoided you, even though that probably made it worse," Heather admitted.

"It did. Which is why I'm ambushing you."

Heather opened her mouth to reply but stopped when she saw Scarlett walking past them. She wanted to stop her, to explain, to introduce her, anything. But all common sense flew out of the window in her panic at her new girlfriend seeing her chatting casually in a dimly lit car park with her ex. Scarlett looked confused but passed by them quickly.

Aurelie turned to watch Scarlett leave.

"Is there a reason why she is looking at us like that?"

Heather pinched the bridge of her nose. "We're dating."

Aurelie's face lit up in a smile. "I see you're going for the younger woman these days?" she teased.

"Yeah, it's a thing I'm trying," Heather joked.

"I wish you both all the best, sincerely," Aurelie said. "I'll go before I cause any more problems."

"I'm sorry—"

"Don't be. Things are the way they are. I hope you have better luck with that one than we did," Aurelie said, turning on her heel and leaving.

Her words sounded genuine, and Heather realised she hoped the same. She hurried up in the hope she would be able to catch up with Scarlett and explain that Aurelie had been waiting for her.

She burst into the centre a few moments later, but Scarlett was already gone. Heather wondered about seeking her out, but thought that might look like a guilty conscience.

Suddenly, she remembered who she was talking about. Scarlett would no doubt ask her directly if she had any concerns. Either way, she made a mental note to bring it up later to advise Scarlett what the impromptu rendezvous had been about.

Just to be on the safe side.

The fact she even considered the potential issue indicated to her how quickly and thoroughly she was already falling for Scarlett.

In many ways, that was a nice problem to have.

Heather stopped by one of her favourite coffee shops, even though she wasn't technically allowed to have a favourite *anything*. She picked up a latte and a porridge to go and headed up to her office.

As she was on the early shift, it was too early for Yasmin to be in, but her office door was wide open and that could only mean one thing.

She breezed into her office and said good morning to Leo.

She'd yet to figure out exactly why Leo was spending so much time at Silver Arches. It had been assumed that he'd quickly hand the reins over to his very competent team and would move on to his next project or acquisition.

But that hadn't been the case.

Either he enjoyed Silver Arches or something wasn't going to plan, Heather assumed.

"Morning," he said gruffly, hardly looking up from his phone as he did.

"Did we have a meeting in the diary?" Heather asked, knowing full well that they didn't. She sat down, turned on her computer, and started to eat her breakfast.

"No. I just needed to run a couple of things by you," Leo said.

He pressed the off button on the top of his phone and slid it into his inner jacket pocket.

"We have all the data back from the various departments, we've crunched the numbers, and we're going to need to make staffing changes. A cut in numbers, nothing too dramatic. Mainly a restructuring, for efficiency."

"Ah, so you're personally telling me I'm fired?" Heather asked with a smile.

It was a joke, but part of her wondered if it was the case. Making light of the situation would ease the conversation if that indeed was what Leo was there to say.

He laughed. "No, definitely not. I couldn't run this centre without you, I know that much."

Heather smiled and continued to eat her breakfast, hoping her relief wasn't too apparent to him.

"You might remember Stephanie Latimer? She was at Audrey's birthday party?" Leo asked.

Heather didn't really remember the woman. She'd met at least a hundred people that night, but she nodded regardless.

"I'm bringing her in. She's great with logistics, knows about leadership and getting the best out of people. Steph's not worked in a corporate environment before, but she knows what she's talking about. She might need a little guidance, but—"

"Do you mean Steph as in Scarlett's ex?" Heather interrupted. The name rang a bell now. An alarm bell.

"That's the one." Leo leaned back in his chair and looked a little cocky. "You're not going to tell me that will be a problem? After your little speech about not accepting people not being able to work together?"

"Not at all. I'll work with whoever you want me to work with. I'm just very surprised that you are bringing her here, all things considered." Heather pushed the rest of her porridge away, appetite lost.

She'd spoken at length with Scarlett the previous

evening, peeling away the layers of supposed indifference until she reached the truth.

Scarlett had been deeply hurt by Steph's words. Even more hurt by the knowledge that Steph seemed to be eager to put everything behind them and now be friends. How could she honestly expect Scarlett to want to be friends after what she had said?

It demonstrated a lack of understanding that what she had said was wrong, Heather thought.

"Relationships break up." Leo shrugged. "If you and Scarlett break up, I assume you'll still be able to work together?"

"Well, of course, that's the nature of dating someone you work with," Heather agreed. "I'm merely a little concerned, what with the way things ended. And the fact that Steph seems to want to forget about it all and pretend it never happened."

Leo sighed. "I don't even know what happened between them; Scarlett doesn't exactly tell me anything. I just know they ended it. Is it really that important?"

Heather took a sip of coffee. "Right, well, it's not really my place to tell you."

"Then we're at a stalemate," Leo said.

Heather held up her hand. "I hadn't finished. It's not my place to tell you, but I will, and if Scarlett doesn't like that, then I'll make it clear that it was my decision to tell you."

Leo folded his arms over his chest. "Go on."

Heather regarded him with curiosity. He looked unperturbed, as if he was about to hear a story about two little girls who couldn't share a hairband.

"She told Scarlett that she was weird; she claimed that she thought she could 'fix her' but realised she couldn't. She told Scarlett that she was too much hard work to be around and that she would never find anyone willing to love her," Heather explained, touching only on the important points. "She utterly broke Scarlett's heart, not just because she ended the relationship but because she made Scarlett feel she was in some way broken and unable to be loved."

Leo's eyes slowly widened. His jaw tensed, and he lowered his hands to grip at the armrests of his chair.

"She said what?" His voice was a cold, harsh whisper.

If Heather hadn't been worried about dating the boss's daughter before, she was now.

"Those are the relevant points," Heather finished, taking another sip of coffee.

Leo leapt out of his chair, causing it to fall backwards. He ran a frustrated hand over his head and stalked over towards the window.

This was the Leo Flynn that Heather had read about in old newspaper articles. The man who made grown men cry. The temper, the throwing of things. She could see it all now.

Heather sat still and quiet and waited for him to calm down. A full two minutes passed of Leo staring out the window with such a force that Heather wondered if the glass might melt.

He slowly turned. "Scratch that plan. Steph will not be coming here. In fact, she'll be looking for a new job."

Heather wanted to argue, not wanting the woman to be fired over a non-work-related conversation regarding a non-work-related incident which had happened a long time ago. On the other hand, she didn't want to stand up for her at all. Steph deserved everything she got.

"I'm sorry." Heather meant it; she was sorry. She didn't want Leo to have to deal with the situation. She didn't want to deal with it herself.

"Well." Leo picked up his chair and righted it. He sat down again. "I suppose I know now."

"You do."

Leo tapped a folder on the desk. "In light of the fact that we won't have Steph on this project any longer, can I run through her report with you now? Just to get your feedback on it."

"Absolutely." Heather was eager to help and also eager to fix Leo's mood.

"Eagle One, report immediately to FC Level Two. Mister Smith. Repeat, Mister Smith."

Heather grabbed the radio from the charging cradle behind her desk and jumped to her feet.

"What's that about?" Leo asked, concern evident in his tone.

"It's code. There's someone in the upper level of the food court with a weapon," Heather explained, already on her way out of her office.

47

The Incident

RAVI STOOD with his arms as wide as he could, members of the public behind him and the knifeman in front of him.

He'd been grabbing a takeaway breakfast when he heard the commotion. Tables were pushed out of the way and chairs clattered to the floor as people tried to get away from the middle-aged man cloaked in a long, black coat.

Ravi hadn't heard what the man was screaming, but he'd seen the knife and quickly radioed it in before starting to do some crowd control.

"Get back!" he shouted to the people behind him.

If the knifeman chose to, he could run at people and cause quite some damage before they could stop him. The centre hadn't fully opened yet, but that only meant that the food court was busy with people getting food and drink while waiting for shops to open their shutters.

"I'll do it! I'll kill you!" the knifeman shouted, seemingly not to any single person. He waved the knife around menacingly; it caught the light and Ravi saw just how powerful a weapon it was.

He'd radioed security first, so he knew they were on the way and that they would have contacted the police. But even if the police rushed, it would be a while before they arrived. It was early morning, with rush hour traffic, and they would have to get to the centre and then to the food court.

Thankfully, workers from various restaurants had jumped over their counters and were assisting Ravi in holding customers back and allowing them to escape the area as quickly as possible. It wasn't lost on him that they were effectively acting as a human shield for members of the public.

Members of the public who were screaming and running around in their attempts to leave the food court through the crowded corridors. Silver Arches simply wasn't built to have a few hundred people all running out of the food court at one time.

"What's the situation?"

Ravi almost sighed in relief at Heather's voice beside him.

"Just this one guy with a knife, no idea what he wants. I was trying to clear the crowd before trying to deescalate. Security have been called and have responded."

Heather put a firm hand on his shoulder and pulled him farther back, taking his place.

"My name is Heather. I'm in charge," Heather called out to the knifeman.

Ravi stepped back, focusing on getting everyone out of the food court while the man was preoccupied. He saw Leo standing next to him, staring at the scene in horror.

"Just another day?" Leo asked Ravi.

"No, I'm as out of my depth as you are on this one," Ravi admitted.

Whatever was causing the hold-up in the corridor seemed to clear, and people started to pour out of the food court and into the main centre. Ravi suspected that security was helping to maintain crowd control.

He looked back at the knifeman and could see Scarlett and Max slowly creeping up behind him. Leo had clearly spotted them, too, as he tensed and took a small step forward.

Ravi grabbed his arm and yanked him back, not wanting Leo to give away their element of surprise.

"Don't look at them," he whispered tersely.

"We can talk about this and get this resolved. I just need you to put down the knife," Heather said calmly, reciting the training they had both received years ago as if she did this every day.

It was times like this when Ravi was pleased he was a deputy and that he had someone like Heather to either take over for or support him where necessary.

A yell echoed throughout the space, and Ravi watched as Scarlett and Max engaged the knifeman. All three were on the floor, and it looked like a scuffle was ensuing.

The knifeman lunged out from underneath them, reaching for the knife that had clattered to the floor. Max grabbed his leg and pulled him back. Scarlett dodged one boot to the face but didn't miss the fist as she crawled to the knife.

Heather leapt over some fallen tables at the same time that Max finally managed to pin the knifeman to the floor. Scarlett grabbed the knife and got to her feet; she picked up her radio from where it had fallen on the ground and announced to her team that the suspect was restrained.

Ravi let out a breath. He turned to face Leo, who was looking ashen.

"Welcome to working with the general public," Ravi said.

48

Not Angry

SCARLETT SAT on the sofa in Heather's office and waited patiently while her girlfriend fussed over the cut below her left eye.

She'd already looked at the graze in the bathroom mirror and decided it wasn't necessary to have it looked at.

Heather disagreed and had spent five minutes gently cleaning it.

Ordinarily, Scarlett would have pointed out that it wasn't necessary, but she found that she enjoyed the attention.

"Don't think this is going to be a frequent occurrence," Heather grumbled.

She'd been alternating between soft and loving words and complaints since they'd arrived in her office ten minutes ago.

"You tending my wounds?" Scarlett asked.

"You getting injured," Heather replied. "This has to stop."

"Should I remind you that I work in security?"

Heather stopped dabbing her cheek with a ball of damp cotton wool and stared at Scarlett. It seemed to be that she was attempting to convey something, presumably something serious.

But Scarlett wasn't getting the message. "What?"

Heather let out a small sigh. She continued to clean the wound, the wound which must by now have been cleaned four times over.

"I was very worried," Heather said.

"Is that why you're angry?"

"I'm not angry. It's just my fear presenting itself as… well, anger." Heather sat back and regarded her handiwork, decided she had done all she could, and placed the used cotton wool ball in the pot of antiseptic cleaning liquid she had been using.

"So, you *are* angry?" Scarlett asked.

"No. Not at you, anyway. It's hard to explain. I had a shock; I thought you were going to get hurt. I'm swaying between wanting to break something and wanting to wrap you in a hug and not let you go."

Scarlett didn't really understand Heather's reaction but found it fascinating regardless.

She'd been doing her job, as had Max. They'd taken down the threat, as per their training. Yes, she had received a minor injury, but it was nothing in comparison to what might have happened.

"Scarlett, about what you saw this morning," Heather started, picking through the contents of a large first aid box and examining various sizes of sticking plaster.

"You and Aurelie in the car park?" Scarlett asked.

"Yes, that. I wanted to say there was nothing going on there. She wanted to talk to me about why she'd come back."

"You're the centre director. It would be hard for her to avoid speaking to you," Scarlett said.

Heather smiled. "Well, I did try. But I just wanted to make sure that you know that there's nothing between Aurelie and me. Never will be."

"You've already told me that."

"Well, I'm telling you again to make sure you understand."

Scarlett didn't know why she needed to be told twice but was satisfied that it was something Heather felt was important.

Heather looked up at her and gently ran her finger under the cut. Scarlett reached up and took the probing finger and placed a small kiss on the tip.

"I'm okay," Scarlett reassured her.

"I know. I will be soon, I promise." Heather leaned forward and softly kissed Scarlett.

It was what Scarlett had wanted from the start, but she hadn't known how Heather would feel about kissing in her office.

The door swung open and Heather jumped back. Scarlett turned to give an evil glare to whoever had interrupted them but stopped dead when she saw her father looking flustered.

"I... sorry," Leo said, averting his eyes as if they were both stark naked rather than sharing the smallest peck of a kiss. "Just wanted to let you know that Ravi and I have dealt with all the police paperwork. You both have to write a statement, but that can be done later."

Heather tidied up the first aid box, closed it, and stood. Scarlett missed her proximity immediately. Leo hesitantly turned back to look at her.

"Are you okay?" Leo asked.

Scarlett nodded. "Yes."

"You're sure?" he pressed.

"I am."

Leo sighed and shook his head. Scarlett regarded him, unsure why her being relatively uninjured seemed to annoy him.

Heather loudly dropped the first aid box onto her desk. "Scarlett's autism means that she generally answers direct questions with a direct answer," she told Leo.

Leo's gaze quickly flicked between Scarlett and Heather.

"Oh." He coughed. "I mean, well, I didn't actually know... that is, well—"

"You didn't know she had autism, I know," Heather said. "Scarlett, do you want to tell your father about your suspicions?"

Scarlett had never told her father of her autism, mainly because she was certain he already knew. Also because she very rarely saw him.

"I believe I'm autistic. I display many of the behaviours. I thought it was obvious," Scarlett explained.

"Well, I had wondered," Leo admitted. "But I didn't know for sure."

"Well, now you do," Heather said. "You two need to learn to talk more."

"We do," Leo confirmed. He approached the sofa and tentatively sat beside Scarlett. "I sometimes find it hard to talk, especially to you."

"Maybe you also have autism?" Scarlett suggested.

Leo and Heather chuckled slightly. Scarlett didn't know why that had been considered funny but didn't mind the lightening of the heavy mood in the room.

"Why don't we go to the pub?" Heather suddenly suggested. "Neutral territory, we can have a chat and a drink. I don't know about you two, but I need one."

"It's half past ten in the morning," Scarlett pointed out.

"Perfect time for a Guinness," Leo said, standing up.

He turned and held out his hand to Scarlett. She took it and allowed him to help her stand. She couldn't remember the last time they had touched one another.

She looked at Heather, feeling a little lost about what was happening. Heather offered her a calming, warm smile, and Scarlett immediately felt safe again.

49

Finally Talking

SITTING in the quiet corner of the local pub, Heather didn't know if she was about to make a bad day better or far, far worse.

She couldn't stand seeing two people so at odds with one another any longer. Leo clearly cared for Scarlett, and Scarlett obviously wanted some kind of relationship with her father. Heather felt for sure that there was a way to bridge the gap.

Of course, there was a possibility that this would all blow up in her face, which was why she had asked for a double whiskey when Leo had asked her what she wanted to drink.

Scarlett shifted uncomfortably next to her, and Heather placed a hand on her knee.

"It will be okay," she promised.

"You don't know that."

"No, I don't. But I have faith."

Scarlett rolled her eyes. "Wishing something will work out is different to it actually working out."

"Doing nothing is a guarantee that it won't work out," Heather countered.

Scarlett didn't reply to that. Heather supposed she didn't need to.

Leo returned with a round tray containing a double whiskey, a large Guinness, and a mug of cocoa. She wondered what the bartender must have thought of such a strange order.

Heather and Scarlett thanked him, and each took a small sip of their drink. Scarlett grimaced, and Heather knew that the cocoa wasn't her preferred brand. Or the temperature was wrong. Apparently, there were a lot of ways to ruin a mug of cocoa.

"Okay, let's cut to it," Heather said. "You two have problems communicating with each other. Let's deal with that."

"I have problems with communicating with everyone," Scarlett pointed out.

"Let's start there. Since when?"

"Forever," Scarlett replied.

Heather turned to Leo. "Do you agree with that?"

"Yes, I think so. Since she was little she struggled to make herself understood. Or we struggled to understand her. We didn't think much of it." Leo took a sip of stout. "Which I now regret."

Heather almost sagged in relief at that. Leo was trying. Reaching out in his own way, owning his responsibility. It was a good start.

"When did things get really bad?" Heather asked.

Leo and Scarlett shared a look. Neither said a word but volumes were being shared silently across the table.

Heather realised in that moment that there had been a flashpoint, a time or an event where everything had changed.

"I'll answer that," Leo said. He took another sip of stout and then pushed the glass to one side. "It was when Scarlett's brother, Ronan, passed."

Scarlett suddenly became interested in drinking her subpar cocoa. Leo examined the woodgrain pattern in the table.

Heather looked from one to the other.

"What happened?" she pushed.

Silence lingered for a couple of beats before Leo looked up. "My first wife, Scarlett's mother, died when Scarlett was four and Ronan was eleven. Scarlett was too young to really understand, but Ronan was hit hard by it. I tried to help him, but I couldn't get through to him. I honestly thought he would grow out of the depressive state he was in."

Leo rubbed his face. "I was a single dad, had a huge business to run. My family helped out where they could, but home life was falling apart. When Ronan was fourteen, he took his own life."

Heather took a sip of whiskey and sagged into her chair. She couldn't imagine the loss of a wife and a child in three short years. Couldn't imagine that kind of loss over the course of even a lifetime.

She looked at Scarlett, realising that she may have only been four when her mother died but she was around seven when she lost her brother. Seven was definitely old enough to remember and understand what had happened.

"I... struggled," Leo admitted after a while. "I found it hard, harder to talk to Scarlett about it."

"We never spoke about it," Scarlett said.

"Not entirely true," Leo argued. "You just... you didn't care. Never once did you show emotion about losing Ronan."

Scarlett ducked her head down. Heather took her hand and held on tightly, willing some strength to flow between them.

"I did care," Scarlett whispered.

"I never saw that," Leo replied. "You never cried. You didn't say you missed him. You... didn't seem to feel anything."

Scarlett shrunk a little at his harsh words, despite the soft tone he'd used.

Heather cleared her throat. "The thing I'm learning, and Scarlett, please correct me if I'm wrong, is that Scarlett seems to show emotions in a different way to you and I sometimes. But that doesn't mean she doesn't have emotions. Isn't that right, Scarlett?"

She squeezed Scarlett's hand, encouraging her to speak.

Scarlett slowly looked up and made eye contact with her father.

"I don't think I feel things in the same way other people do," she confessed. "But I miss Ronan. He was my brother and I loved him. But he's gone and talking about him won't bring him back."

"I know that," Leo defended himself.

"But you spent a lot of time trying to make me talk about him when I was a teenager," Scarlett explained.

"And then became angry when I couldn't."

"I wanted to make sure you remembered him," Leo said. "And... I suppose I wanted to prove to myself that you did feel something about his loss. Scarlett, you were the only kid I ever heard of to go through their teenage years without a single tantrum, crying fest, crush, anything. You were just... emotionless."

Heather held up her free hand. "There's a difference between being emotionless and showing those emotions in a different way to what you're used to."

Leo nodded. "Yes, I realise that now. But at the time, I just... I felt so angry. And then every time we spoke... I didn't know if I was getting through."

"I didn't say much because when I did speak, it seemed to make you angry," Scarlett confessed.

Leo opened his mouth and then slammed it shut again. He picked up the stout and took a couple of sips.

"I'm sorry, Scarlett," he finally said. "I know that your childhood wasn't exactly a happy one. I wasn't there, and when I was... I wasn't a very good father."

"You were a good father," Scarlett disputed. "You kept me safe, sheltered, fed. I never wanted for anything."

Heather couldn't help but place a soft kiss on Scarlett's cheek. Almost anyone else would have agreed immediately that they had endured a hard childhood and that Leo had been absent or emotionally unavailable.

But Scarlett didn't hold a grudge; in fact, she honestly seemed to believe that Leo had been a good father to her. Even when the evidence Heather had gathered indicated otherwise.

Leo stood up and sat on the bench beside Scarlett and

swept her into a bear hug. Scarlett seemed slow to react, probably shocked by the action. Heather wondered how long it had been since they had hugged.

"I love you so very much," Leo said firmly. "I'm sorry that I've been a terrible father."

"I'm sorry that I've been a terrible daughter," Scarlett replied.

Heather rolled her eyes. "No one has been a terrible anything," she told the ridiculous pair. "You both need to learn to communicate and understand that you are very different personalities."

Father and daughter slowly pulled apart, but Leo kept his arm around Scarlett's shoulder. "I'm going to do my best," he promised.

Scarlett's phone beeped from its location on the table. She picked it up and glanced at the screen. "Tara wishes to see me; I have to go."

Scarlett stood up and started to walk away. A moment later she turned and came back to the table.

"I'm glad we spoke. And I hope we will again very soon," she said to her father. She turned to Heather. "I'll miss you; I will call you later."

Before either could reply, she turned and left again. Heather couldn't help but chuckle. It was progress, but Scarlett's goodbyes still needed a little work.

"She's always done that," Leo said, reaching for his stout. "Just upped and left. It's not often that you even get a goodbye."

"I spoke to her about it last night," Heather confessed. "I said it might be considered rude by some if she just leaves without a word like that."

Leo regarded Heather with a crooked grin. "You've really managed to get through to her, haven't you?"

"Maybe a little, but the key has been to adapt my behaviour rather than to think she should adapt hers," Heather explained.

"I'd like to learn that," Leo said.

"The first thing I learnt was that, if you want Scarlett to speak to you in more than one or two words at a time, you have to ask her a proper question," Heather said.

"I think sometimes I didn't like her answers," Leo admitted.

"She's different to you and me," Heather said again. "And you have to take that into consideration. But she's smart, dedicated, and she does care a lot about things. Once you really start to look."

Leo smiled and took another sip of stout. "Maybe you two can come over for dinner one night soon? I'll even promise to not talk about work. Much."

Heather felt a blush on her cheeks. She realised that Leo had very astutely noticed that she was falling for Scarlett and that their relationship was fast moving to a personal one.

"I'd like that," she said. "I'll ask Scarlett how she feels about it."

"Good." Leo's phone rang and he rolled his eyes. "Well, had to happen eventually."

"I suppose it did," Heather agreed. "I'd best get back to the office anyway."

"Good job today," Leo said as Heather started to get up. "You dealt with that incident like it was any other day.

Not that I ever had any doubts, but it was good to see that my centre is in safe hands."

Heather smiled and nodded her thanks. She wouldn't mention that she had been terrified and shaking like a leaf throughout the experience. That could be her little secret.

50

You Were Right

SCARLETT ENTERED Silver Arches and started to make her way up the stairs towards the offices. She could see Ravi ahead; she hurried a little to catch up to him.

When he noticed her, he slowed down and looked at her with a wide smile.

"Hey, Scarlett, you doing okay?" he asked.

"Yes. I wanted to talk to you," she said. "I wanted to tell you that you were right, and I was wrong."

Ravi frowned. "You've lost me."

Scarlett wasn't surprised by that. She often lost people when she started a conversation.

"You once said that if something doesn't work out then it's because something better is around the corner," Scarlett reminded him. "At the time, I disagreed with you. On reflection, I think you were right."

Ravi paused on the stairs and grinned. "Oh really?"

"Yes."

Ravi regarded her with a look she couldn't quite place.

He looked happy, but then the deputy centre director always appeared to be happy.

He put an arm around Scarlett's shoulder, and they continued to climb the stairs.

"I'm really glad you're at Silver Arches, Scarlett," he said, giving her a small squeeze.

"I'm glad to be here too," she confessed.

He removed his arm from her shoulder when they got to the top of the stairs. They each opened one half of the double doors leading into the management suite and stepped inside.

"You're becoming quite the local hero," he told her.

Scarlett actually snorted a laugh at that comment.

"Unlikely," she said.

"It's true," Ravi told her.

"I'm not a hero. I was doing my job," Scarlett said.

"It doesn't matter what you think; it matters what they think," Ravi said. He subtly gestured around the corridor.

Staff members were looking at her, and many were smiling at her. Scarlett couldn't remember the last time these people had actually made eye contact with her. She wasn't unaware that she had made a number of enemies since she started at Silver Arches. It wasn't her intention, but it had been the unintended result of her actions.

It happened nearly everywhere she went. She somehow made enemies, and before long she had no idea how to turn the tide.

Whenever she started in a new department, she never had any aim of trying to make friends because it always seemed like an impossible mountain to climb.

Now she wondered if maybe she could.

She offered a tentative smile back to people as they passed.

Maybe Silver Arches could be a family to her, as Heather so often described it.

51

Four Minutes Late

HEATHER WAITED at Ore station with her hands in her jeans pockets. Scarlett's train was running four minutes late, and each minute seemed like an injustice, carving into the amount of time they would be spending together that day.

Of course, she couldn't really complain. They had been dating for three weeks and seen each other quite frequently. In fact, it felt like they had been together for far longer.

Something had clicked between them, and their relationship felt comfortable while also remaining new and exciting.

At her father's request, Heather had agreed to spend the weekend with her parents in Hastings, and Scarlett's adorable pout had prompted her to issue an invitation. To her delight, Scarlett jumped at the chance to spend more time with her and to meet her parents for a second time.

Her father had already enjoyed plenty of jokes at Heather's expense now that she finally admitted that not only was she interested in Scarlett, but that they were happily dating.

Sue had nudged him in the ribs and looked at Heather fondly, stating that she was very happy that Heather had found someone.

Heather had to admit that she was very happy too. Happier than she could remember ever being before.

The train pulled into the station. Heather tried to play it cool and look calm, but she knew in her heart that she looked how she felt: eager.

It had been two days since she'd laid eyes on Scarlett. They'd exchanged text messages, but it wasn't enough.

The train doors opened, and a handful of people disembarked, including Scarlett.

Heather stepped forward and raised her arm so Scarlett would see her.

"My train was delayed," Scarlett greeted her.

"I know."

"Four minutes. A signalling fault," Scarlett continued.

Heather grinned. "I know. Can I have a kiss hello?"

Scarlett's expression changed in a flash from annoyed to delighted. She ducked her head and pressed her lips to Heather's. Heather let out a pleased sigh.

"I've been waiting forever for that."

"I was only four minutes late," Scarlett pointed out.

"I've not seen you for two days," Heather grouched.

"Do you miss me that much?" Scarlett asked, sounding slightly perplexed.

"I do. Very much," Heather confirmed. "Do you miss me?"

Scarlett considered the question for a moment. "Now and then."

Heather burst out laughing. She'd walked right into that one. She took Scarlett's hand and led her towards her father's Jeep.

"When I allow myself to think about it," Scarlett added. "Then I miss you. So, I try to not think about it. I'd always rather be with you than without you. That much is obvious to me now."

Heather stopped dead and stared open-mouthed at Scarlett.

"Have I said something wrong?" Scarlett asked.

"No." Heather swallowed. "No, I think you just said the most romantic thing I've ever heard."

Scarlett beamed.

Heather kissed Scarlett's cheek, wanting to do more but already knowing her father would accuse them of lying about the delayed train and having spent the time making out in the car instead.

"I love you," Heather said. It had taken her less than a week to say the three small though significant words to Scarlett. It was faster than she ever had said them before, but the words also held more meaning than they had ever held before.

Scarlett had said them back immediately with the widest smile Heather had ever seen on her face.

Heather didn't know how she had managed it, but at some point, she had not only managed to crack the mysterious code that was Scarlett Flynn. She'd also found the woman of her dreams.

Epilogue

"I'll miss this little cube," Nico said, patting the side of her pop-up shop wistfully.

Ravi lifted a heavy box of books onto an existing stack of boxes on a heavy-duty trolley.

"The centre won't be the same without you," he admitted.

"I know. They have big shoes to fill," Nico agreed. "This place was incredibly dull without me; I can sense that."

Ravi chuckled to himself. "It was. I mean, I had no idea that Hot Dog Boy was living a lie. Serving hot dogs all day every day and actually being allergic to them."

Nico nodded sagely. "And every time someone asks him for a personal recommendation from the menu, he has to lie. Pretending he has tried them all, when one bite would land him in hospital."

"I didn't even know people could be allergic to hot dogs," Ravi admitted.

He lifted another heavy box, wondering why he always

did Nico's heavy lifting while she just fiddled with stickers or fondly patted the side of her temporary store.

"Ah, there you are!"

Ravi saw Leo Flynn coming over and stopped what he was doing, expecting that the man was coming to speak to him. He was surprised when Leo passed him and approached Nico.

"Hey, Mister Flynn," Nico greeted.

"I read that proposal you sent over to my office, and I like it. I like it a lot," Leo told her.

Ravi's eyebrows lifted.

"I thought you might." Nico got her business card from her back pocket and handed it to Leo. It was rainbow-coloured and had a glitter heart on the back. Ravi knew because he was still finding glitter everywhere from the one Nico had given him four months ago.

"Get in touch and we can arrange a meeting," Nico told him.

Leo took the card and nodded. "I'll definitely do that." He turned and glanced at Ravi. "Good night, Ravi. See you tomorrow."

"Night, Leo," Ravi said, looking at the retreating figure in confusion. He looked back at Nico. "What was that about?"

"I did a little research, and Intrex are seriously lacking in some rainbow credentials. I put a proposal together, pointing that fact out and explaining my business plan to bring my LGBTQ books to the masses." Nico shrugged casually. "Man knows a good business proposal when he sees one."

Ravi folded his arms and regarded his friend with a grin. "So that's why you've been researching him."

"Of course. You think I'm going to let an opportunity like this go to waste?" Nico asked him.

"You're smarter than I am, Nico," Ravi admitted.

"Yeah, I am," Nico said with a playful wink. She turned. "Aww, look at that."

Ravi looked up and smiled at the sight of Scarlett and Heather walking hand in hand through the centre.

"How long's it been now?" Nico asked.

"Five weeks, I think," Ravi said. "Heather's head over heels."

Of course he was still teasing Heather mercilessly about it. That was the kind of brother/sister relationship they had. In truth, he couldn't be happier for her. It had been a long while since Heather had been with someone, and he'd never seen her as happy as she was now.

Somehow, Scarlett was the perfect fit for her. Ravi never would have believed it if he hadn't seen it for himself.

The pair approached, and Heather pouted at Nico.

"It's going to be so odd without you here," Heather said.

"I know, I was just saying to Ravi how boring it must have been without me," Nico said.

Heather laughed. "It was. I don't know how we managed."

Nico got her phone out of her pocket. "Right, group photo. Come on, gather round, everyone."

Nico's arms were too short to get them all in the shot,

so Ravi took the phone and the four of them stood in front of the Gay Days pop-up and posed for a photo.

After the shot was taken, Nico checked it and looked up at Scarlett.

"Hey, you're smiling," Nico told her.

Scarlett grinned and replied, "Of course I am. I'm happy."

P
12/7/23

Patreon

I adore publishing. There's a wonderful thrill that comes from crafting a manuscript and then releasing it to the world. Especially when you are writing woman loving woman characters. I'm blessed to receive messages from readers all over the world who are thrilled to discover characters and scenarios that resemble their lives.

Books are entertaining escapism, but they are also reinforcement that we are not alone in our struggles. I'm passionate about writing books that people can identify with. Books that are accessible to all and show that love—and acceptance—can be found no matter who you are.

I've been lucky enough to have published books that have been best-sellers and even some award-winners. While I'm still quite a new author, I have plans to write many, many more novels. However, writing, editing, and marketing books take up a lot of time… and writing full-time is a treadmill-like existence, especially in a very small niche market like mine.

Don't get me wrong, I feel very grateful and lucky to

be able to live the life I do. But being a full-time author in a small market means never being able to stop and work on developing my writing style, it means rarely having the time or budget to properly market my books, it means immediately picking up the next project the moment the previous has finished.

This is why I have set up a Patreon account. With Patreon, you can donate a small amount each month to enable me to hop off of my treadmill for a while in order to reach my goals. Goals such as exploring better marketing options, developing my writing craft, and investigating writing articles and screenplays.

My Patreon page is a place for exclusive first looks at new works, insight into upcoming projects, Q&A sessions, as well as special gifts and dedications. I'm also pleased to give all of my Patreon subscribers access to **exclusive short stories** which have been written just for patrons. There are tiers to suit all budgets.

My readers are some of the kindest and most supportive people I have met, and I appreciate every book borrow or purchase. With the added support of Patreon, I hope to be able to develop my writing career in order to become a better author as well as level up my marketing strategy to help my books to reach a wider audience.

https://www.patreon.com/aeradley

Reviews

I sincerely hope you enjoyed reading this book.

If you did, I would greatly appreciate a short review on your favourite book website.

Reviews are crucial for any author, and even just a line or two can make a huge difference.

About the Author

Amanda Radley had no desire to be a writer but accidentally became an award-winning, bestselling author.

She gave up a marketing career in order to make stuff up for a living instead. She claims the similarities are startling.

She describes herself as a Wife. Traveller. Tea Drinker. Biscuit Eater. Animal Lover. Master Pragmatist. Procrastinator. Theme Park Fan.

Connect with Amanda
www.amandaradley.com

Also by Amanda Radley

Going Up

2020 Selfies Finalist

A ruthless executive. A destitute woman. Both on the way up.

Selina Hale is on her way to the top. She's been working towards a boardroom position on the thirteenth floor for her entire career. And no one is going to get in her way. Not her clueless boss, her soon to be ex-wife, and most certainly not the homeless person who has moved into the car park at work.

Kate Morgan fell through the cracks in a broken support system and found herself destitute. Determined and strong-willed, she's not about to accept help from a mean business woman who can't even remember the names of her own nephews.

As their lives continue to intertwine, they have no choice but to work together and follow each other on their journey up.

Also by Amanda Radley

Second Chances

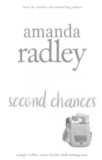

Bad childhood memories start to resurface when Hannah Hall's daughter Rosie begins school. To make matters more complicated, Hannah has been steadfastly ignoring the obvious truth that Rosie is intellectually gifted and wise beyond her years.

In the crumbling old school she meets Rosie's new teacher Alice Spencer who has moved from the city to teach in the small coastal town of Fairlight.

Alice immediately sees Rosie's potential and embarks on developing an educational curriculum to suit Rosie's needs, to Hannah's dismay.

Teacher and mother clash over what's best for young Rosie.

Will they be able to compromise? Will Hannah finally open up to someone about her own damaged upbringing?

And will they be able to ignore the sparks that fly whenever they are in the same room?

Also by Amanda Radley

Lost at Sea

A stowaway. A perceptive captain. Both drawn together.

Annie Peck finds herself in a terrible situation and is literally running for her life. A chance encounter with a surprising lookalike leads her towards a risky solution.

Captain Caroline West knows she is lucky to be one of the few women cruise ship captains in the world. Sadly, not having a standard nine to five job means relationships are nearly impossible and she's all but given up on finding anyone.

Join these two women for an all-expenses-paid cruise of the Mediterranean and find out what happens when an identity thief with a heart of gold meets the rule-abiding woman who could throw her in jail.

Copyright © 2020 Amanda Radley

*All rights reserved. No part of this book may be reproduced in any form on by
an electronic or mechanical means, including information storage and retrieval
systems, without permission in writing from the publisher, except by a reviewer
who may quote brief passages in a review.*

*This is a work of fiction. Names, characters, places, and incidents either are the
product of the author's imagination or are used fictitiously. Any resemblance to
actual persons, living or dead, events, or locales is entirely coincidental.*

Made in United States
Troutdale, OR
11/20/2023

14760628R00202